She found herself watching his lips.

It was crazy. And yet somehow she needed to feel something besides this stifling fear and overwhelming outrage. She needed to feel anything but that.

"I need you to hold me, Krueger." She hadn't meant to say out loud what she felt. But she needed this too badly to pretend she hadn't meant the words.

He didn't hesitate. Those strong arms went around her and pulled her close against his chest. Claire laid her cheek there and closed her eyes. When his hands started to move slowly over her back, she could feel the urgent pull of his desire and knew for certain she wasn't in this alone.

Dear Reader,

Thank you so much for picking up my newest Silhouette Bombshell novel, *Staying Alive*. Writing this book was a pleasure, and I hope you'll enjoy reading it as much as I enjoyed writing it.

During the process of bringing these characters to life I wrote some of my own past into the story. My sister and I became estranged many years ago. For more than a dozen years we did not see each other or even speak. It was a dark time in my life. Like Claire and Whitney in this story, a tragic event brought my sister and me back together. We shared our regrets, and we cried our hearts out and in the end I had my sister back.

Also, like Claire Grant, I grew up in small-town Alabama. I hope you will enjoy Claire's story. And if you can take one thing away from this story, please take this: love is far stronger than anything on earth...all you have to do is let it guide you.

Very best regards,

Debra Webb

Debra Webb

STAYING
ALIVE

Published by Silhouette Books

America's Publisher of Contemporary Romance

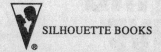 SILHOUETTE BOOKS

ISBN-13: 978-0-373-51438-0
ISBN-10:   0-373-51438-7

STAYING ALIVE

Visit Silhouette Books at www.eHarlequin.com

Printed in U.S.A.

Selected Books by Debra Webb

DEBRA WEBB

was born in Scottsboro, Alabama, to parents who taught her that anything is possible if you want it badly enough. She began writing at age nine. Eventually she met and married the man of her dreams, and tried some other occupations, including selling vacuum cleaners, working in a factory, a daycare center, a hospital and a department store. Later, with the support of her husband and two beautiful daughters, Debra took up writing again, looking to mystery and movies for inspiration. In 1998 her dream of writing for Harlequin Books came true. You can write to Debra with your comments at P.O. Box 64, Huntland, Tennessee 37345 or visit her Web site at www.debrawebb.com to find out exciting news about her next book.

The characters in this book are very special to me. The events that take place between these sisters were drawn from a very real place in my heart. This book is dedicated to Mary Ann, my beloved sister. I thank God every day that I have her back in my life.

Prologue

"The transport is set for 1:00 p.m. tomorrow."

Habib Nusair absorbed the information without comment though the news was not what he had hoped for. There was no time for second-guessing now.

From his high-rise apartment he stared out over the city of Seattle, Washington, his hatred searing through him with such force that he shook with the roar of it.

This had been his mistake.

His miscalculation.

But he would right that grave injustice no matter the price.

Today.

"Assemble a team of four to include me," he said to the man who waited nervously for his response. "Our timing must be precise. There is no margin for error."

"Habib." The man who served as his personal advisor moved closer. "The risk is far too great. Allow me to serve in your stead. You know I will not fail you."

Habib glared at him, anger snarling inside him. "No. *I* will make this right. I will not bring shame on my father's name by sending someone else to right my wrong."

His confidante humbly bowed his head. "Of course. I will inform the others that our retaliation is imminent."

Habib turned his attention back to the view beyond the glass. He would strike quickly with a blow that would bring the imperialist pigs to their knees.

He had waited his whole life for a moment to shine outside the shadow of his father.

Now the time was at hand.

No matter that the coming strike had been motivated by an error in judgment, he would ensure that his error evolved into a monumental turning point for the cause.

He would not fail.

Chapter 1

Claire Grant cradled her cup of coffee and inhaled deeply of the rich aroma. She closed her eyes and relished the heavenly scent.

Five minutes of peace in the teachers' lounge. That was all she needed.

Everything had gone wrong this morning, starting with a soggy trip to school. The rain would do her flowers good, but it did nothing for her mood.

From the arrival of her first student until the fourth-period bell rang and the group filed down the hall for art class, she hadn't had a moment of quiet time to herself. To make matters worse, it was Monday. No one wanted to be at school on Monday, especially not a room full of fifth graders. They wanted to sleep in as they had done on Saturday and Sunday. Plus, Saturday-morning cartoons were far more entertaining than math, history and science.

Claire wasn't immune to the curse of Blue Monday herself. She couldn't remember the last time she'd slept in…until this weekend. Now she, too, paid the price. Her usual patience had thinned far too early in the day for comfort, hers or her students. And the day was scarcely half over.

Maybe this cup of coffee and a few minutes of peace and quiet was all she needed and she would be good to go. She hoped.

The entire fifth-grade wing was now gloriously silent. The rooms, even the halls, were absent of the usual noises of running feet and teasing banter. The next forty minutes were not to be taken for granted.

The first sip of caffeine-infused heat was no letdown. The savory brew tasted every bit as good as it smelled. Darlene Vernon must have made this pot. No one at Whitesburg Middle School made coffee the way Darlene did. Claire felt certain that whoever created Starbuck's had lifted the house recipe from Darlene. Claire had to smile when she considered the probable name the popular coffee house chain would have ended up with had Darlene been the one to conceive the idea. Something like Brewing with Darlene or the Grind, she imagined. Her friend had a fiercely wicked sense of humor for a middle-school teacher.

Speak of the devil.

"I hope your morning is going better than mine," Darlene noted, that famous sense of humor apparently having gone temporarily dry.

All fifth-grade students spent fourth period in one of three places, physical education, art or music, giving the teachers a free period for planning and, usually, a much-needed break. It looked as though Claire wasn't the only one extra thankful for the respite today.

Claire leaned against the counter next to the coffee station and shot her friend a challenging glance. "Would you like to compare war stories?"

Darlene fired back one of those skeptical looks, her eyebrow arching upward like a ticked off cat's back. "Matthew Pearson cut off both of Tessa Mott's braids." She faked a smile. "I win."

"You're right," Claire admitted, stunned, "you do win." She sipped her delicious coffee, trying not to imagine poor little Tessa's shock at seeing her waist-length braids on the floor.

"Poor you," Claire mused, suddenly realizing the rest of the story. "You have to tell Tessa's mother."

"Tell me about it. Maybe I'll change my name and run away," Darlene said dramatically.

A new kind of tension flared but Claire tried to ignore it. She didn't have to tense up any time changing names and running away was mentioned. Darlene knew nothing about that part of Claire's life. Her comment was in no way personal. She and Claire had been friends for a long time. Claire was just being paranoid.

Darlene poured a cup of coffee and took a swallow before changing the subject. "Did you hear about that big takedown this weekend? It happened at the University Village." She leaned in close. "Yours truly was there." Another of those eyebrow-raising looks followed the statement. "I saw the whole thing happen. It was really freaky."

Claire racked her brain for some memory of a big news event over the weekend. She finally lifted her shoulders in admission of her failure to stay abreast of current events. "Sorry. I spent half the weekend sleeping in and the other planting spring flowers." The reality sounded even more pathetic out loud.

Darlene glanced around covertly as if what she had to say was top secret, then she tugged Claire farther from the door. "Hamid Kaibar. He's on some kind of top ten terrorist watch list. Undercover agents pounced on him right in front of the Pottery Barn."

Claire felt a frown working furrows across her brow. "Do they have a top ten list?" Okay, she obviously didn't stay up to speed on that sort of thing to the extent that her friend did. But this sounded like something she should know.

Darlene rolled her eyes. "Duh. They have all kinds of lists. Anyway, this guy is supposedly connected to, like, the most infamous, evil terrorist on the planet. Abdul Nusair. Surely you've heard of him."

Claire definitely recognized that name. She nodded. "I've heard of him." She didn't follow the whole terrorist business too closely in an effort to ensure she slept at night. It was simply too disturbing. She was happy to leave it to her government to take care of the situation. She had faith in those she elected to office.

Still, with one of the top ten terrorists in the world captured in Seattle, at a mall near the Washington University campus at that, she probably should do a better job of keeping up. She did vaguely recall hearing that border states such as the one in which she lived were particularly vulnerable to the risk of terrorists slipping in undetected. She felt certain the government had taken additional precautions in those states. A couple of local politicians had voiced concerns, she remembered now that she thought of it. State

Representative Reimes had been very vocal about it in a number of forums. Some of the teachers had suggested that he might not get himself re-elected if he kept pushing the boundaries about terrorist profiling. Not that they discussed politics regularly but Reimes's son attended Whitesburg Middle.

"Apparently," Darlene said, "sometime tomorrow they're transporting the prisoner to some secret facility where he'll be properly interrogated. Mr. Allen thinks he may be the key to capturing Nusair."

Dale Allen was the principal of their school. A former social studies teacher, he liked staying in the know on the subject of world events.

"That should make his friends a little nervous," Claire suggested. "I wouldn't want to be the one responsible for asking him questions."

Darlene indulged her thirst for more caffeine before going on. "It makes me wish I'd bought some protection years ago. And learned how to use it properly," she added, her tone uncharacteristically somber.

"Sometimes that can do more harm than good." Claire really hadn't meant to make the comment but it was out of her mouth before she could stop it.

"And just what would you know about the subject? As I recollect, I was the one who had to chase that bird out of your classroom a week or so ago. I believe your excuse was something like 'I'm afraid I'll hurt the poor thing.'"

"I grew up in rural Alabama," Claire reminded her. This wasn't exactly the kind of childhood memory one shared with anyone other than close friends. "My father insisted that his offspring know how to handle a rifle for protection as well as survival reasons."

Darlene's eyes widened. "By survival you mean hunting, right? For food. As in stalking Bambi in the forest?"

Claire rolled her eyes. "I never stalked Bambi. But yes, I mean hunting. It's a Southern thing."

A devilish grin spread across her friend's face. "Like your accent."

"I don't have an accent anymore," Claire argued, unable to actually get annoyed at the other woman's teasing. Darlene loved ribbing Claire about her Southern accent. All her friends did. "I'll have you know that five years in Seattle has all but abolished any hint of my Southern roots."

An incredulous laugh danced across Darlene's lips as she freshened her coffee. "You just keep telling yourself that, darlin'."

Claire cleared her throat. "I may have a slight Southern intonation, but my diction is impeccable. I never leave off the *G* in *i-n-g*, darling."

Darlene laughed again. "Oh, touchy, touchy."

The insistent, high-pitched shrill of the fire alarm shattered the silence in the hall outside the lounge. Well-honed instincts launched Claire and Darlene, as well as every other teacher in the wing, into action.

Double-checking the rooms to confirm all was as it should be, then locating their students and ensuring they evacuated the building as quickly and safely as possible came as much second nature as breathing.

"I can't believe this," Darlene huffed as they hustled along the empty corridor and through the double doors that led to the fine arts section at the far end of the wing. "Why would they have a fire drill when it's raining outside?"

The hurried steps of the other teachers in the corridor echoed behind them. "Maybe it's not a drill." Claire's pulse rate accelerated at the idea. Though they were well prepared for most any type of emergency, no teacher looked forward to the possibility of a *real* emergency. Too many things could go wrong. Too many variables to name when dealing with children. One mistake, one oversight, could cost a precious life.

Claire caught sight of Mrs. Patricia Talley, the art teacher, and hastened her step to catch up with her class. "Hey, Pat." She surveyed her students and smiled at the other woman. "Is this a drill?"

Pat shrugged her thin shoulders. She was the tiniest woman, scarcely five feet tall, with a full head of gray hair despite being only in her early forties. "I sure didn't hear anything about it if it is."

Claire glanced around the building as they exited. She didn't see any sign of smoke. Didn't hear any approaching sirens outside. Surely it was a drill, but generally the staff received advanced warning. Apparently someone had forgotten to mention this one.

Rain or no rain.

And it was definitely still raining.

The children didn't seem to mind, however. They laughed and turned their faces up at the sky to allow the big drops to splash noses, open mouths and joyous, dimpled cheeks.

Claire hustled along, counting heads as the nice straight line of students marched across the inner courtyard toward their designated safe place. She felt proud as she counted heads along the way. Her kids were reacting exactly as trained.

She mentally acknowledged each little face as she counted. Eighteen. Nineteen.

Wait.

She paused, surveyed the faces again. There were supposed to be twenty. No one was absent today unless a student had been checked out during this period, which had scarcely begun.

Uneasiness trickled through her.

"Pat, did one of my students check out?" The urgency of the question had Claire's heart slamming mercilessly against her sternum. She mentally skimmed the names until she landed on the one whose face she had not seen in the line. Peter Reimes.

Pat shook her head. "I don't think so. We had just settled down to take roll when the alarm sounded. Who's missing?" She scanned the row of students as they reached their destination near the flagpole in the front quad beyond the drop-off entrance.

"Peter," Pat said more to herself than to Claire.

Fear expanded in Claire's chest. She rushed over to Vance Richardson. "Vance, where is Peter?" The two boys were almost inseparable.

Vance looked a little nervous. Rain dripped down his cheeks like tears. Claire experienced a quake of dread at his hesitation.

"Where is he, Vance?"

She had to find that child *now*.

"He didn't want to paint today, Miss Grant." Vance scrubbed at the water slipping down his face. "He said he was too tired. He was going to hide in the restroom and maybe take a nap."

Christ. Claire turned to Pat who had come up behind her. "I'm going back in for him."

"No." Pat shook her head vigorously. "I'll go back for him. You stay with the kids."

"He's my student," Claire reminded. "You stay."

Not waiting for any more of Pat's resistance, she raced across the drop-off lanes and the inner courtyard. Her blouse and slacks were beginning to plaster to her skin. Her ponytail was drenched as well but she didn't care. If there was any chance whatsoever that this drill was real—even if it wasn't real—she had to find that child.

She couldn't imagine why he hadn't come out of hiding when he heard the alarm. The students were instructed over and over again on the proper response to the sound of that alarm.

And then she knew.

He was too tired to paint and wanted to take a nap.

Peter was diabetic. His blood sugar had probably dropped too low. He could be unconscious in that bathroom. If the alarm hadn't gone off, Pat would have called roll by now and she would have noted his absence and sent someone to look for him.

Not only could he be in grave danger assuming the alarm was real, if his sugar level had dropped that low, every minute counted.

The long, empty main corridor in the fifth-grade wing felt ominous…as if certain doom was about to descend. She had to find that child.

"Miss Grant!"

Claire had just turned left toward the corridor

leading to the art room when her name resounded behind her. She twisted around to face Principal Allen. "Sir, I'm—"

"You should be outside with the others," he cut her off. "What're you doing back in here?"

The material plastered to her skin and the water puddling around her feet confirmed his assumption that she'd already been outside. "I'm missing a student."

The words rang in the ensuing silence. Words no teacher ever wanted to utter. It was the worst-possible scenario under any circumstances. That there could possibly be a fire in some part of the school only increased the urgency.

The whiteness of fear overwhelmed the red flush that had appeared on Mr. Allen's face during the hurried evacuation efforts. "I'll radio for additional assistance."

"Let's check the boys' bathroom first. He's probably there." She was already moving in that direction as she spoke. "I'm worried about his sugar level. If he were conscious I'm sure he would have come outside when he heard the alarm."

It wasn't impossible that he was outside amid the throng of students. A couple of minutes were required for every single student to be counted. If so, someone would notice that he was out of place and escort him to his own group.

Just when her heart was about to rupture with fear, Mr. Allen's walkie-talkie crackled. "Mr. Allen, Claire Grant is inside the building looking for Peter Reimes. Let her know he's with his group now. He came out with the music class."

Relief rushed through her and her knees wobbled just a bit. "Thank God."

Mr. Allen, acknowledging the reaction, patted her shoulder gently. "It's all right now. You get back to your group and I'll finish checking this wing."

She nodded. "Yes, sir."

Claire trudged back outside, ignoring the continuing drizzle.

However bad she'd thought her morning had been, the rest of her day had just taken a major bad turn. Even the mere thought of losing a child tore her apart…made her second-guess the most basic of her teaching skills.

Darlene offered her a hang-in-there smile across the damp quad as Claire rejoined her students.

She surveyed her group and said a silent prayer of thanks as she caught her breath. The kids were okay and that was all that counted in the end.

By two that afternoon her world was back to normal. Claire doubted her blood pressure would be back below stroke range anytime soon, but it would fall eventually. The mere idea of having one of her students left inside the building during an actual emergency situation still took her breath away. It would be days before she stopped obsessing on the horrific notion.

Thank God there hadn't been a fire or any other threatening situation.

The alarm had reacted to an anomaly in the system, whatever that meant. All Claire knew for certain was that it hadn't been a planned drill; it had been a mistake.

Peter had bounced back after a carton of apple juice. As she suspected, his sugar level had dropped and he'd put off taking care of the situation until he briefly lost consciousness. He didn't like that he needed to monitor his levels. A typical man in the making, he assumed he could get through the low without asking for help.

With less than an hour to go, her students, who had all changed from their damp clothes into their gym attire, had settled back into their work. Instead of reading aloud this afternoon, she'd decided to have quiet, individual reading time. She could catch up on the lesson planning she'd missed during the unintended fire drill.

Like her, most of the teachers kept a change of clothes at school. Working with kids this age had taught her long ago to expect most anything.

Her hair, much to her dismay, had coiled into its natural abundance of unruly curls. The ponytail barely restrained the wild mass. She spent at least a half hour every morning smoothing the kind of mane others paid stylists top dollar to create.

Not Claire. She had always hated her naturally curly hair. Almost as much as she loathed her full figure. It wasn't that she was fat, exactly. Darlene called her curvaceous.

Claire worked out. She really did. And she ate right...except for the chocolate. It was her one major downfall. There were far worse bad habits, she reminded herself on a regular basis. And, the fact of the matter was, all the women in the Grant family were healthy-sized...so to speak.

You couldn't fight genetics.

Scuffling in the hall snapped her back to the present and jerked her head up. She was on her feet and moving toward the door before the possible sources of the sounds fully penetrated. Once in a while some of the boys came to blows, but not that often. She was shocked that anyone had been allowed in the hall long enough to get into trouble after the watery fire drill.

She turned the knob and pulled the door open far enough to ease out of the room. She'd just gotten her students settled. Whoever was making all the ruckus was going to get a glimpse of her less-than-pleasant side. "What's going on—?"

The rest of the words evaporated in her throat as her brain analyzed what her eyes saw.

Two men wearing black ski masks had Mr. Allen trapped against the wall, a gun to his head.

Fear throttled through Claire. Before her brain even gave the order she had already pushed the door closed behind her in hopes of somehow protecting her students.

An arm came around her throat and jerked her backward against a hard body.

"Don't make a sound."

The threat was whispered against her ear.

Her gaze met Mr. Allen's and she saw the extreme fear that mirrored her own.

"Bring him into this room," the man holding her ordered.

The two thugs jerked Mr. Allen away from the wall and started toward Claire.

…this room.

They meant her room.

"No. We can't go in there. My students—"

Fingers twisted in her hair and yanked her head back. "Shut up!" he hissed in her ear.

Her captor opened the classroom door and shoved her inside.

"Lay your heads down!" Claire ordered, barely

catching herself from the momentum of his brutal push. She didn't want her kids to see this. The terror she felt was nothing compared with what their impressionable minds would experience. "Lay your heads down!" she repeated. The longer she could put off their panic the better.

Heads went down onto folded arms. She let go a ragged breath and thanked God that they had obeyed quickly enough that they wouldn't witness the horrible scene unfolding around them. The three masked men entered the room with Mr. Allen in tow. Claire kept a close eye on her students, hoping their curiosity wouldn't have them peeking.

She should have known better than to hope.

"Down on the floor," the goon in charge growled to Mr. Allen.

A single gasp ignited a rush of wide, curious eyes peeking above little arms.

That was when the screaming began.

Chapter 2

Claire moved from student to student attempting to calm them down.

The man who appeared to be in charge pointed at her. "You. Come here."

He leveled his weapon on her as she approached. It was difficult for her to draw in a breath, much less put one foot in front of the other.

When she stopped about four feet away she looked him straight in the eye. "Yes?" Somehow her anger had overtaken her fear. Or maybe she'd gone numb or stupid with the business end of that automatic rifle pointed at her heart.

Whatever it was, she hated this man for scaring the children like this.

What kind of animal terrorized children?

"Move everyone to the back of the room."

He gestured to the area behind the children's desks, where a long window that filled most of the wall looked out over the inner quad. Claire blinked in disbelief. She hadn't noticed until then that the police were already on the campus. Beyond the inner quad, just past the drop-off point, at least a dozen official vehicles had gathered in the front courtyard of Whitesburg Middle School.

She turned back to the man doling out the instructions and nodded her understanding. He was taller than the other three, but slight, not nearly as heavily built. His voice, though mean and uncaring, sounded young.

"Line up as many of the children as possible on the window stool with their backs to the room. Do what you must to keep them quiet."

Her heart thumped hard at the oddness of his request. "Why?"

Cold black eyes glared at her. "Do it or die."

Somehow the order to move made it from her brain to her legs and she took the necessary steps to follow his order. As she moved back across the room she glanced at Mr. Allen. One of the masked men had

secured him to the chair behind Claire's desk with
what looked like yellow nylon rope. The bindings
were clearly too tight. Her heart went out to him.

What did these men want? Why were they doing this? Why her school?

She scolded herself for letting the questions
splinter her attention. She had to keep her head
about her.

One by one she ushered the children to the back
of the room. "Help me move the projects and
plants, okay?" She had lined the window stool
with plants that the children helped water and
projects that had been completed recently.

"What's happening, Miss Grant?" Kira Hall
stared up at her, her hazel eyes round with worry.
"Why are those men wearing masks and holding
guns?"

"I'm not sure, Kira. Let's just do what they tell
us to do and be very quiet. I think everything will
be okay if we do that."

Claire prayed she wasn't lying to the child.

Please, God, don't let this turn out badly.

Once the window stool was cleared, she
assisted one child after the other onto the wide
marble ledge. "Face out the window," she told
them quietly. They would be better off not seeing
whatever was about to happen in this room.

By the time she'd reached the other end of the

window, her entire class stood on that ledge staring out at the cluster of law enforcement vehicles.

Claire chewed her lip. Maybe this was worse than sitting in their desks staring at those men. She just didn't know. Seeing those police cars out there would only alarm the children all the more.

"You!"

She pivoted to look at the man, the one she presumed to be in charge.

"Come here."

"Stay very still and quiet, boys and girls," she said once more, her voice as soothing as she could make it. Then, with a deep breath for courage, she walked back to her desk where the three men waited.

"Go through each backpack and purse, including your own, and remove any cellular phones. Bring them here to me."

Few of her students had cell phones but she knew she would find one or two. She nodded. "All right." Her gaze met the principal's briefly as she turned to do her captor's bidding. The image of the children lined up in that window, their backs turned to the hateful intruders, had her stomach dropping to her feet.

It was at that exact moment that she realized the purpose of putting the children in the window.

The realization made her heart follow the path her stomach had already taken.

The window stool was about forty inches off the floor and the window towered another five feet above that. There were no drapes or blinds to draw.

He was using the children to block the view into the room. And, probably, as a reminder of what was at stake. No way could a sniper attempt to take out any of the bad guys with the children lining the window. It was too risky.

These evil men had considered every contingency.

But why?

As she checked the backpacks hanging on a line of hooks mounted on the wall that divided her room from the hall, she wondered again why this school had been chosen. Why her classroom? Was it simply because she'd stepped into the hall at the wrong time? Or was there some other reason she just didn't comprehend yet.

Peter Reimes. A new jolt of fear shook her. His father was a state representative who took an aggressive stance on fighting terrorism. His name and face would be known to men like these. His family would be an easy target.

She couldn't be sure…but it was the only theory that made sense so far.

The men spoke perfect English. Were these men terrorists in the most-prevailing sense of the word or were they just thugs?

By the time she'd reached the final backpack she'd discovered five cell phones. Her first instinct was to keep one. Somehow attempt to hide it in the pocket of her slacks. But if she was discovered, it could cost her more than she wanted to pay. The way things looked, it wasn't like she would get the opportunity to use it. The chances of all three men stepping out of the room at once was about nil and if she turned on the phone and entered 9-1-1, the operator's voice would give her away. And that wasn't even counting the one man watching her every move. She might not be restrained the way Mr. Allen was, but she by no means had free rein. The leader knew the best way to use her to keep the children quiet. If she appeared under control, the children would respond better.

So she took the phones and placed them on the desk. She purposely avoided going around behind the desk to get the one in her purse. Maybe he wouldn't notice that she hadn't done that. Maybe he would assume her purse had been in one of the backpacks. Plenty of teachers carried back-packs, too.

"Remove the one from your purse," he in-structed when she met his gaze.

So much for that plan. She crouched next to Mr. Allen and reached into her purse. She took the phone and placed it on the desk with the others.

"What do you want me to do now?"

He gestured to the window filled with children. "Stay close to your students. Ensure that no one makes a mistake that would get him or her killed."

Fear barbed ruthlessly. Still, she managed a nod before going off to do his bidding. Right now co-operation was essential.

Resuming her position in the row of children, who remained surprisingly quiet, Claire turned to face her desk. She didn't want her back to these men. Whatever happened next, she wanted to see it coming.

The man giving all the orders used the muzzle of his weapon to slide Claire's phone across her desk to Mr. Allen. "We're going to make a call and you're going to do the talking for us. Do you understand?"

Mr. Allen nodded, the movement jerky.

Claire thought about how he'd had a heart attack last year. The red blotches amid the pallor of his face had her worried. But what could she do?

Nothing.

The man in charge nodded to one of his associates who picked up Claire's phone and entered a number before placing the phone against Mr. Allen's ear.

"Identify yourself and state your situation."

"This is Principal Dale Allen from Whitesburg Middle School," he said. "Approximately twenty fifth-grade students, a teacher, Miss Claire Grant, and I have been taken hostage by what I believe to be a group of three terrorists."

Shock rumbled through Claire. Terrorists? She looked at first one man then the next and the next. Were these terrorists promoting some cause or was this about money? Were they foreigners? She couldn't see their faces. Their voices sounded as American as her own. She'd already considered the concept that this was a terrorist act…but somehow hearing Mr. Allen say it made it more real. Mr. Allen kept up with the ongoing terrorist threats of the world. He would have a better grasp than she.

What could they hope to accomplish for their cause at her school? It didn't make sense. Kidnapping a state representative's child wouldn't carry the kind of worldwide leverage terrorists usually went after…would it? Sure, the Reimes name was one associated with antiterrorism, but was that enough to cause these men to promote their agenda in this manner?

She surveyed the students to ensure no one had turned to face the threat or had moved out of position.

"Tell them," the man instructing Mr. Allen went on, "that we wish to speak directly with State Representative Paul Reimes."

Reimes. Claire's gaze settled on the back of Peter Reimes's head. So they were here about him. Again, she wondered if this was a kidnapping gone wrong. Maybe they weren't terrorists. Maybe this was about money.

Mr. Allen repeated the demand as instructed.

Claire's attention shifted from the boy to the scene playing out at the front of the room.

"The secretary says State Representative Reimes is out of the office but they're trying to track him down."

Claire's heart bumped into a faster rhythm. What would these men do now? She sidestepped, taking her time so as not to draw the attention of the third man who now loitered in the middle of the room watching his comrades. She stopped dead in her tracks when he turned to survey her and the children.

When he turned back to his friends, she moved right a couple more steps until she stood directly in front of Peter Reimes.

"Find him," Allen echoed the leader's words. "Tell him to call this number immediately." Mr. Allen blinked, looked confused a moment. "She wants to know what number she should call."

The leader swung his cold gaze toward Claire. "What is the number?"

She called out her cell number without hesitation.

Mr. Allen repeated it.

The man holding her phone closed it, ending the call.

"Very good, Mr. Allen," the man—no, the *terrorist*—in charge offered. "Continue to do exactly as I tell you and perhaps you will survive this day."

Claire felt herself tremble. She tried to suppress the reaction but she couldn't keep her body still.

This was not the kind of event you survived.

Oh, God.

"Where are the other kids going?"

Claire pivoted to the boy who'd spoken. Several of the other students began to talk all at once and point out the window.

"Quiet, boys and girls." She strained to see the scene outside. Sure enough, children from the rooms in the rest of this wing were pouring across the quad. They rushed to meet the policemen.

Not just policemen, SWAT team members. Claire recognized the all-black combat gear, including the helmets. The realization that SWAT had been called in confirmed what she had already concluded.

They were going to die.

No. She squared her shoulders and refused to allow another tremble. They were not going to die.

These were children. She scanned the poor

kids watching their schoolmates run to safety. She couldn't bear the thought of even one of them being hurt.

The door to her classroom flew open, drawing her thoughts back to the front.

"The other rooms have been cleared," a fourth man dressed in black and wearing a ski mask announced. He closed the door and, rather than join his friends at Claire's desk, remained at the door.

Were there more or was this it? Each man was armed with an automatic rifle. The fourth man spoke with the same smooth English as the others, maybe just the slightest hint of an accent but too vague for her to identify.

"Miss Grant, I'm tired."

She spun quickly to scrutinize Peter Reimes who looked sickly pale. "Did you take your medicine this morning?" Usually he didn't have this much trouble keeping his level steady.

He nodded. "But I still don't feel good."

All the excitement was having an adverse affect on his blood-sugar level. He would need food or juice.

"I don't feel good either," Penny Myers echoed.

Claire had to get this chain reaction under control before every single child started complaining. Antagonizing these men would not be helpful to their situation.

"Settle down, boys and girls. We have to be very quiet," she said firmly.

She patted Peter's arm. "I'll find you something to snack on. That should help." Then she turned to face the front of the room. "This child," she said, deliberately not mentioning his name, "is diabetic. He needs a snack. May I look in the backpacks for something edible?"

The man in charge gestured to his cohort, the one standing in the middle of the room keeping an eye on Claire and the kids. The man strode over to where the backpacks hung and started rifling through them.

Claire's cell phone vibrated, making a grinding sound against the top of her desk.

"Answer it."

One of the goons picked up the phone, opened it and held it against the principal's ear. "This is Principal Allen." He looked up at the man who gave the orders. "It's State Representative Reimes."

The other man finished searching the backpack and abruptly thrust a pack of snack crackers at Claire. Her hand shaking, she reached out and took the small package. "Thank you."

The man didn't respond. He stalked back to his position. She quickly opened the crackers and passed the package to Peter. Then she moved down the length of the window and made soothing comments to the rest of her students in hopes of keeping them calm. As she did, she took every opportunity to survey the goings-on beyond the drop-off area.

Were they planning a rescue attempt?

How in the world would they be able to do that? There was no access to the room other than the one door and this one long window. The emergency exit was actually an operational section of window at the southeast corner of the room. The rest of the window was sealed shut. Even if someone managed to open that emergency exit, no more than one or two of the children would be able to escape before the man watching them noticed.

Right now, the best thing to do was to stay cool and not to make any moves that could be considered aggressive or uncooperative.

The leader's demands drew her full attention back to the front of the room.

"You have just one hour. If the authorities do not release Hamid Kaibar by then, your son will die. Another child will die every half hour after that until Kaibar is released."

Terror wrapped around Claire's chest and tightened to the point of making breathing near impossible.

Surely it wouldn't come to that.

Surely the authorities would comply with their demands.

And release a terrorist? Darlene's words about Hamid Kaibar reignited in her brain. One on the top ten list?

It was at that precise moment that Claire fully understood the ramifications of their predicament.

Her first assessment had been correct.

They were going to die.

"I want my mommy," Lila Miles whimpered. Her plea set off a cacophony of similar sentiments.

"Let's settle down, girls and boys," Claire urged, desperation taking deep root at this point.

"Miss Grant!"

The brutal tone made Claire flinch as she faced the man in charge.

"Control your students or I will do it for you."

She knew exactly what that meant.

Turning back to the window lined with children, she shouted, "Quiet, now!"

She moved along the row, touching each student with what she hoped would be a reassuring gesture while urging them to be calm. She promised that all would be fine, that they would be going home soon.

She prayed her promises would not prove to be lies.

"Representative Reimes says that one hour is not enough time."

Mr. Allen's voice shook with the impact of the

message he had no choice but to relay. Dread twisting into tiny knots in her stomach, Claire waited for a response from the men at the front of the room.

"One hour is all he has," their captor stated. "That hour started five minutes ago. That is all I have to say."

Mr. Allen repeated the statement into Claire's cell phone and the man holding the phone closed it, severing the connection.

Claire worked for several precious moments to maintain her composure as she whispered soothing assurances to the children. Remaining calm was absolutely essential. If there was any hope at all of devising an escape plan, she could not be distracted by panic or fear.

There was no way the authorities were going to release a terrorist, not even to save these children. Claire almost lost hope then and there. The police would try to help. Representative Reimes would call in his every marker, put the pressure on the political chain of command. But she knew all too well what would happen if the powers that be decided to have SWAT converge on the classroom in lieu of releasing the prisoner.

There would be few survivors.

It wasn't that she didn't trust the highly trained members of such an elite force to do the best job possible, but the four gunmen holding her class captive had nothing to lose. If they went down they would want to incur as much collateral damage as possible. Even if tear gas were somehow introduced into the room to disable the terrorists, they would go down firing those automatic weapons. The children were lined up in the window like sitting ducks in a carnival shooting gallery.

They would be the first to die.

She glanced at the clock high on the wall above the white board behind her desk. In forty-five minutes, the man in charge had promised, the first child would be sacrificed if his demand was not met.

She had to figure out a way to stop that from happening.

Her gaze landed on Mr. Allen. There was nothing he could do. He was bound securely with a masked guard towering over him. The leader lingered around the desk as well. Waiting for the call back, she supposed.

The other two men were covering the door and the classroom at large, including her and the children.

Four armed men and all these children.

She had no weapon, no actual training in how to fight off an attacker. Sure she'd taken a self-defense course once. But that course had focused mainly on preventing the possibility of sexual assault. She had no idea how to fend off terrorists.

One thing she did know, however, was how to fire a weapon. She was no expert by any means. She wasn't even a particularly good shot. But she knew how a rifle worked. All she needed was to get her hands on one and then she'd just shoot until they didn't move anymore, as her father had always put it.

If he were still alive, her father would be proud of her for attempting to assess her options under the circumstances, but even he would have to admit that her chances of accomplishing anything were sorely limited. Still, she had to try. Giving up was not her style.

She considered the items she had seen in the children's backpacks when she'd gone through them. The phones had all been turned over as requested. There really hadn't been anything else she could use as a weapon. Getting into her desk was out of the question.

What could she use as a weapon? Her gaze skimmed the array of projects the children had turned in last week. A miniature volcano. A papiermâché dinosaur. A Pterosaur complete with nest and hand-painted eggs. The model of the prehistoric bird was fairly large with pointy metal claws about the size of ink pens attached to its feet. The bird was mounted on a stand as if flying over its nest. If she could pretend to knock it off the desk, she could pull one of the claws free as she picked up the mess. Then use it as a weapon, if she got the opportunity. It wouldn't be much, but it was better than nothing.

Claire checked on her students. They were getting restless. She moved from one to the other and urged them to keep their eyes on the police cars no matter what happened and to stay quiet. When she'd again reached the row of desks where the Pterosaur sat she backed up a couple of steps and started to turn. Just as she'd planned, she bumped into the bird's widespread wings and knocked it off balance.

The bird and stand crashed to the floor.

The aim of four weapons fell on her.

"I'm sorry."

For three or four seconds, she couldn't catch her breath. She was sure one of the men would shoot her where she stood.

As if God had been watching out for her, her cell phone vibrated against her desktop, drawing all attention there.

Relief flooded her and somehow her heart started to beat once more. She took a deep breath.

While the men focused on the call, she crouched down and started to gather parts of the damaged bird. She pulled loose one of the pointy claws and slid it into the right pocket of her slacks while keeping an eye on the terrorists. When she'd placed the broken bird back atop the desk, she stood.

Mr. Allen's face had gone utterly white.

Even from across the room she could see the sweat dampening his forehead.

The phone was crushed against his ear so that he could listen to what the caller had to say.

He looked up at the terrorist in charge. "Representative Reimes has tried everything he knows to do but the federal authorities will not release Mr. Kaibar. But he would like to offer the four of you a chance at freedom in return for the lives of the children."

"Tell him," their captor said, his voice cold, "that we will not bother to wait the final fifteen minutes. His son dies now."

Mr. Allen repeated the information, his face now going a sickly gray color.

Claire stood, unable to move, and watched this moment play out. Her mind kept recapping the same words over and over.

They were going to kill the children, starting with Peter.

Mr. Allen abruptly gagged, then gasped for air.

"Mr. Allen!" She moved toward him before her mind registered what she was doing.

Weapons took aim at her, but she couldn't stop.

"Stay with the children," the man in charge ordered.

She hesitated long enough to glare at him. "He has a bad heart. He could be having a heart attack! I have to help him!"

The leader nodded to his cohort, the one who'd handled the phone.

Before Claire could reach her desk, the man had shoved her chair, Mr. Allen still bound to it, into the corner. He leveled his weapon and fired.

The blast exploded in the room and left an ugly round role in the center of Mr. Allen's chest. Blood oozed down his shirtfront.

Claire screamed and ran toward him.

One of the goons stopped her.

She fought to get free but he was too strong.

The children cried in the background. She should go to them. She knew she should but she couldn't take her eyes off poor Mr. Allen.

The leader walked over to her. He grabbed her face in one ruthless hand. "Bring me the Reimes boy," he snarled to the man restraining her who immediately let her go.

This was it. The moment of no return.

She had to do something…if she could just break free.

Fear and hurt churned desperately inside her. But there was nothing she could do for Mr. Allen now. She had to try and help the children.

"Not the children," she blurted, the leader's hard fingers still digging into her skin. "Kill me instead."

He laughed. "So, you want to be a martyr?"

"Kill me," she urged, scared to death he wouldn't agree and at the same time worried that even this wouldn't stop him from harming the children. Surely the SWAT team was prepared to take action considering a weapon had been fired. As much as she feared the results of that…it was better than nothing. At least some might survive. "Kill me instead of the boy. Please."

The leader laughed long and loud. "We'll let our martyr be the one to pull the trigger."

A new surge of terror made her sick to her stomach, had her knees threatening to buckle beneath her.

The leader leaned his face close to hers. "Have you ever killed anyone, sweet teacher?"

"Stop!" She tried to get free but her attempt proved futile. "I won't do it."

"You'll do whatever I say," he growled, his voice savage.

As the others watched, the man snatched Peter

Reimes from the window and moved back toward the front of the room. The children cried frantically. Claire's heart shattered at the idea that she couldn't protect them. There was nothing she could do.

"It's okay, boys and girls," she cried, despite the ringleader's brutal hold on her chin. "I want you to keep watching out the window."

Her heart squeezed painfully when every last one obeyed. Still, their soft whimpers made her want to kill these four men with her bare hands.

By the time the man dragging Peter shoved him toward the leader, her entire body trembled violently. She couldn't make it stop.

Oh, God. Oh, God. Please don't let this happen.

As the leader released her, the man who had brought Peter forward manacled her around the waist with his left arm and slammed her hard against his body. He forced her hands onto his rifle.

"Please," she cried. "No!"

The leader gripped Peter's shoulder with his left hand and used his right to manipulate and then press the barrel of his comrade's rifle against the boy's forehead.

"Wrap her finger around the trigger," the leader ordered. "Make her do it! Now!"

"No!" The word tore out of her throat on a wave of anguish.

Tears slipped down Peter's reddened cheeks. "I want my mommy," he pleaded, then cried out as his captor wrenched his shoulder harder.

There was nothing she could do to stop this.

The man restraining her with his left arm used both hands now to force hers to do as his leader had ordered.

"That's better," the one in charge said softly, lethally as her finger was stuffed into place.

Her teeth ground together and she wished more than anything in the world that she could kill this subhuman creature.

"I'm going to count to three, teacher, and then we're going to do this. I want you to have time to look into the boy's eyes before you kill him. One…two…"

"Screw you!"

In a move the man restraining her had not anticipated, she pulled back hard on the rifle's stock, jerking the barrel out of the leader's hand. Without missing a beat, she twisted left with all her might as her right forefinger coiled against the trigger. The weapon fired, sending a bullet straight through the chest of the man holding Peter. His gaze held hers for one eternal instant before he crumpled to the floor.

"You stupid bitch!"

The man restraining her yanked the rifle free of

her reach. Her right hand dived into her pocket and grabbed the metal claw. As he tried to shove her away, she jammed the claw into his thigh with every ounce of force in her body.

He howled with pain.

She threw herself onto Peter, taking him down to the floor.

Glass shattered and some kind of foul-smelling smoke suddenly filled the room.

More shots echoed in the air.

She could hear the children screaming.

Chapter 3

"Step away from the weapon!"

Claire huddled behind her desk, Peter in her arms, as three men dressed in SWAT gear faced off with the only terrorist left standing. As soon as SWAT had stormed the classroom, she and Peter took the closest form of cover.

The children were crying on the other side of the room. God, she needed to get to them. But she had been ordered to stay put. She understood that the one remaining terrorist was still armed.

She peeked around the corner of her desk. The smoke was slowly clearing. Two other guys in

SWAT garb were trying to see to the children. But as far as Claire was concerned, the kids needed their teacher.

Moving wasn't an option. She couldn't risk getting in the way of the ongoing standoff. Staying put was the hardest thing to do, but reason told her that any distraction could have devastating consequences. So she resisted the desperate urge to go to the children.

The three men suddenly converged on the lone terrorist. When he was cuffed, Claire scrambled to her feet. "I need to go to the children now," she said to no one in particular. Her heart pounded so hard she could scarcely hear herself think.

"Go ahead, ma'am."

She waited until they had ushered their prisoner to the door and then she reached for Peter. "Come on, Peter, let's go see about the others."

"You are dead!"

A chill rushed over Claire's skin at the savage sound of the prisoner's voice. She turned toward the man who had issued the threat. He resisted being ushered out the door. His mask had been removed and he glowered at her with sheer hatred.

"You are dead!" he repeated, his tone imbued with violence.

Claire knew in that instant that, if given the opportunity, this man would kill her where she stood.

SWAT muscled him out of the room.

The children's cries dragged her attention back to the matter at hand. She shook off the creepy feeling the man's threat had evoked. He was going to prison just like his friend Kaibar. He wouldn't be giving anyone else any trouble.

As Claire made her way past the nearest terrorist, lying in a pool of blood on the floor, a SWAT team member, in an effort to check ID, tugged off the dead man's mask. Claire froze. Her gaze riveted to the face of the man she had killed.

Definitely Middle Eastern and probably no more than twenty or twenty-one years old.

Not much more than a kid himself.

A sick feeling churned in her stomach.

She had killed this man.

Her gaze moved across the room to the other two downed terrorists. It had scarcely been more than an hour since this horror began and four men had lost their lives. She looked back at poor Mr. Allen and she felt her own tears well up all over again.

Such a horrible, horrible way to die.

The sobbing pleas of the children continued to fill the air. They were shaken and afraid, they wanted their parents. She couldn't let her own distress hold her back from providing the support her students needed.

Claire sucked up her courage and hurried across the room, weaving around chaotic fallout. She had to be strong for the children. She couldn't think about anything else right now.

During the hour or so that followed, paramedics examined the children. Thankfully they were all fine. A few had received cuts from the flying glass and minor scrapes and bruises from having fallen or jumped off the window stool when the smoke canister blasted through the window above their heads. Some were treated for mild cases of smoke inhalation, but otherwise they were all amazingly unharmed and ready to go home.

"Ma'am, I'll need to examine you now."

Claire looked up as the paramedic approached her. "Don't bother. I'm fine," she argued.

She might have some bruises come tomorrow, but otherwise she was okay.

"I'm sorry, ma'am," he coaxed, "but I have orders. I have to take a look. Make sure you're uninjured. Sometimes a mild case of shock will veil other problems not readily visible."

She was too tired to argue and he did have his orders. "Do whatever you have to."

Claire leaned against her desk and let him do a quick screening. Her blood pressure and heart rate were a little high, but that was to be expected. The paramedic evaluated her from head to toe. He was kind and patient.

"You appear to be fine, ma'am," he acknowledged. "But I would suggest that you see your private physician if you suffer any residual effects."

She frowned. "What do you mean, residual effects?" She was tired and maybe even a little grumpy.

"You might require something to help you sleep for the next couple of nights. These things sometimes take a toll not always apparent in a routine physical exam."

Counseling. He meant trauma counseling and sedatives. She'd been down that road before.

"I understand." He was right. The children would certainly need professional help. Coming back to school would present a scary experience in and of itself. Perhaps Mr. Allen…

Claire swallowed hard, tried her best not to start crying again.

At some point, an hour or so after the shoot-out, the children were allowed to go home with their emotionally fatigued parents. Claire stood at the entrance door to the fifth-grade wing and watched each shell-shocked parent pick up his or her child. She offered whatever reassurances she could, but there wasn't a lot she could say that would make anyone feel better just now.

When the last of the children were gone, a man in a suit approached her. He didn't look familiar, but she'd seen so many faces she very well could have met him already. "Miss Grant, I'm Detective Vince Atwood." He showed her his official ID. "I need to ask you a few questions now."

She followed him into the classroom across the hall from her own. As she passed her open door she caught a glimpse of the young man she'd killed being lifted into a body bag. She shuddered.

She'd killed a man today.

She had hoped that she would never have to feel this way again. That fate would not demand such a tragic act from her twice in one lifetime.

Detective Atwood ushered her to the chair behind her colleague's desk, then he settled one hip on the desk's edge. As she watched he removed a small notebook from his pocket and flipped it open.

"Miss Grant, I'd like you to tell me what happened, starting with the fire drill."

Claire started slowly. Her thoughts were a little jumbled at first, but eventually she reconstructed the events leading up to the moment when the glass shattered and the smoke filled her classroom.

Detective Atwood explained that as soon as gunfire had been confirmed SWAT was given the order to storm the room. Sending in the smoke bomb had been about providing cover for their entrance. They had already infiltrated the room with audio and visual devices, using the ventilation system. SWAT had known exactly where the children were as well as where each terrorist stood before they entered the room, ensuring a surgical strike with, fortunately, no collateral damage.

"You understand, Miss Grant, that you may be required to answer questions several more times. In cases such as these where children are involved as well as threats to national security, there are a number of levels of accountability. Child Services may require a full report on the incident. Certainly, the state school system will need to understand what occurred in an effort to comprehend any needed steps that might prevent such an incident in the future. The Federal Bureau of Investigation and Homeland Security may require interviews as well."

"I'm happy to do whatever I need to," she assured him.

Detective Atwood closed his notebook and tucked it back into his jacket pocket. He heaved a heavy breath. "Miss Grant, I regret the need to bring this up, but it's my job. We ran background checks on both you and Mr. Allen while we were…waiting and…well, I have just a couple of questions on a flag that came up on your history."

Claire stilled. The past came barreling in to

collide with the present. She should have seen this one coming, but she'd been a little busy and a whole lot terrified for the past couple of hours.

"Six years ago you were involved in another shooting," the detective began, clearly hesitant to bring up the subject. "There was some confusion, as you've changed your name since."

"That's right." The idea that anything related to that nightmare would come into play in this act of terrorism made her want to scream at the injustice of it. But she reserved judgment. As the detective said, he was only doing his job. "I kept my last name," she said. "I wasn't running from the law, Detective, I simply needed the anonymity of leaving Christina Grant behind."

When Atwood didn't immediately launch into another question, Claire decided to save them both any further awkward moments. "My younger sister married a jerk," she said, cutting right to the chase. "He made her life miserable. He was both mentally and physically abusive. During the final months of her pregnancy she came to live with me to get away from him."

"She was afraid for her life as well as that of her unborn child," Atwood said, clearly regurgitating what he'd read in her official police record.

Claire nodded. "One night he broke into my house. He had a gun. When he tried to kill my sister, I charged him. We struggled. The weapon discharged and he died."

Atwood nodded. "That's what the report said." His gaze met hers. "Word for word."

Something like doubt flickered in his eyes and Claire resisted the impulse to defend herself further. She had done what she had to do that night…she'd done it again today. God knew she hadn't had any choice in either situation. As far as she was concerned that was good enough for her.

She couldn't regret the actions that had saved the lives of innocent people.

"Is there anything else, Detective?" She stood. Her legs were still a little unsteady, but she wanted out of here. The sooner the better.

Atwood shook his head.

When Claire was about to walk away, he said, "Just so you know, Miss Grant…"

Reluctantly, she turned back to him. She didn't want this to be a warning not to leave town. She'd weathered far too much gossip and suspicion six years ago. She shouldn't have to tolerate it now, especially considering the reason for today's events.

"You did the right thing," Atwood allowed. "Then and now."

The sincerity of his words was reflected in his eyes. All signs of doubt or suspicion were gone.

Any resentment or irritation she'd felt ebbed

away. She nodded and resumed her retreat. She wanted to go home. She was completely exhausted. A long hot bath and sleep were the only two things on her agenda.

Darlene waited for her in the hall. "Are you okay?" She rushed up and hugged Claire. "God, I was so scared."

Claire held on to her friend, thankful to be alive. "I can't believe this happened."

Darlene drew back and gave her a smile. "You did good, girlfriend. You saved those kids. Don't let anybody tell you differently. I was out there." She jerked her head toward the front of the building. "They didn't know what the hell they were going to do to save you guys. No one thought there would be any survivors."

Claire's knees buckled this time. Her friend caught her. "Let's get you home," Darlene suggested. "I'll get your car to you later."

"I need my purse."

Darlene banged on Claire's classroom door and had one of the officers bring her purse out of the room. Her classroom was now a crime scene awaiting thorough forensics investigation. When her purse was in her hand, Claire wasn't surprised to find that it had been thoroughly searched. But what came next was something else Claire should have seen coming but didn't.

Reporters. Hundreds of them.

The police had cordoned off the school at the drop-off point, but beyond that there were literally hundreds of reporters. Dozens of television vans.

Claire lost count of how many teachers praised her for holding her own in an unwinnable situation. She tried to keep her smile in place but it wasn't easy.

A couple of officers showed up and escorted Claire and Darlene through the crowd. It seemed as if half the community had come to observe the events. The children had all been picked up, but most of the teachers remained. Several were openly mourning the loss of their beloved principal.

Camera flashes seemed to punctuate the questions hurled at her. She ignored them all. She had nothing to say. Not to the media anyway.

Darlene opened the door of her racy red sports car for Claire and then hurried around to the driver's side while the police kept the reporters at bay.

As they drove away, Claire stared at the school growing smaller and smaller in the rearview mirror. Nothing would ever be the same there. Today's horrendous events would forever leave a mark on the teachers as well as the students.

And for what?

She just didn't get it.

Why couldn't someone stop the terrorists, their senseless demands, their murder of innocent people?

She laid her head back against the headrest. Maybe because they were all like her, sitting back leaving it to someone else. She wasn't sure she would ever be able to watch the news and feel the same way again. Maybe that was the problem with the world today, everyone passed the buck, put the dirty work off on someone else. She would never again take for granted the efforts of her country to fight terrorism.

Firsthand experience was a ruthless teacher.

Her eyes closed in a futile attempt to erase the image of the man she had killed today. An image from the past abruptly superimposed itself over his.

She forced the painful pictures away. She would not regret what she had done. Both of those men deserved to die. She hated that she'd been the one forced to stop them, but it was done.

There was no going back.

"You want to stay at my place tonight?"

Claire cleared her head of the disturbing thoughts. "Thank you, but I think I'd feel better in my own bed."

She closed her eyes again and focused on making her body relax. First that tight band of tension around her skull, then the aching tendons reaching down her neck. She let her shoulders slump downward. She was so tired. So exhausted.

Claire hadn't realized she'd dozed off until the car stopped moving. She hadn't exactly been asleep but she'd floated in that place between asleep and awake.

"You're sure you're okay, Claire?"

She faced her friend and produced a smile. "I'm okay. I'll see you in the morning."

Darlene shook her head. "No school tomorrow. Maybe not the next day."

Of course there wouldn't be any school. The investigation would need to continue. Her classroom would need repairs. And Mr. Allen. God, poor Mr. Allen. There would be arrangements for his memorial service.

"I'll talk to you later then." Claire opened her door but hesitated before getting out. "Thanks, Darlene. I don't think I could have driven home after…"

Darlene placed her hand over Claire's and squeezed. "I know. Call me if you need me, no matter the hour."

Claire emerged from the car and waved as she watched her friend drive away. She felt a little numb. She hadn't noticed that before. Maybe the reality of the last few hours was only now beginning to catch up with her.

Glancing down the block, first left then right, she was immensely glad no reporters had found out where she lived. She doubted that would last, but at least they weren't here now.

She turned and faced her small bungalow. It wasn't much. Just a one-bedroom, one-bathroom fixer-upper she'd spent the last five years transforming, but it was home and she loved it.

As she took her time advancing along the sidewalk, she focused on the details of her home. Anything to clear her head of the ugliness. She loved the Craftsman-style bay window that looked out over her front yard. She'd just planted lots of flowers last weekend. With April coming to a close the colorful, lush annuals were starting to bloom, the reds, yellows and purples brilliant against the pale green of her house and the rich brown of the eucalyptus mulch.

She had a white picket fence, a detached garage and her own little garden toolshed in the back.

So far, she had done good, if she did say so herself.

Stepping up onto the covered porch, she admired her swing. She'd layered it with comfy cushions. She loved sitting out here reading with a cup of coffee on Saturday mornings. Her house faced east, so she could watch the sunrise as well.

It was perfect for her. Felt like home in every way.

That was something she hadn't expected when she moved here. She had missed Alabama so badly, but she'd needed a fresh start. When she'd found this place, it had been in pretty sad shape. Like her.

Claire unlocked the door and went inside. She'd spent all summer that year transforming the exterior into a showcase of curb appeal. Then, during those long dreary winter months that followed, she had, inch by inch, revitalized the interior. From the period crown molding to the rustic tile in the light-filled kitchen. She'd had to hire someone to do the wiring update. Most older homes didn't meet the current code.

But that overwhelming kitchen renovation was all that had gotten her through her first Christmas alone.

"Enough."

Claire sat her purse on the table next to the door and engaged the dead bolt. She allowed the familiar smells and textures of home to soothe her as she walked toward the bathroom, shedding her clothes as she went. By the time she reached the bathroom she'd stripped down to her panties and bra.

While the original claw-foot tub filled with steaming hot water, she fashioned her unruly blond curls into the closest thing to a bun she could manage in this condition.

Big, dark smudges beneath her brown eyes made them look sunken. The first trace of bruises on her upper arms and throat had begun to surface. Good thing the weather was still cool enough for

a long-sleeved turtleneck. Otherwise she'd look…
just like her sister used to. She shivered at the
images that resurrected.

Banishing the memories, Claire poured her
favorite scented oil into the tub and inhaled
deeply as the luxuriant lavender essence infused
the rising steam.

She stepped into the tub and slowly lowered
herself into the welcoming embrace of the hot
water. After turning off the tap, she leaned back
and let the neck-deep water do its work.

It felt so good. The heat penetrated her muscles
and urged them to relax. The steam filled the
room, creating a cozy cloud of thick, damp silence.

She didn't need any music or candles. Just this
glorious heat and the blessed silence.

The phone rang, the muffled sound reached beyond the barrier of the door, cut through her cozy
cloud, but she refused to open her eyes. She was
way too exhausted to care who might be calling.

Probably some of the other teachers checking
up on her. The teachers were her family now. They
had accepted her as one of their own. She received
an invitation to every birthday, every wedding and
funeral just as if she had always been here.

This was home.

The past was over and done with. No going back.

No looking back.

That was the hardest part. When things happened to provoke an old memory…like being forced to shoot that man today…she couldn't help wondering. But going back was detrimental to her well-being. She could not think about the past and continue to be happy in her present.

End of story.

And just like that, the images of the terrorist she'd killed flashed one after the other in her head. His harsh words. His unflinching brutality. He would have killed little Peter Reimes with no compunction at all. How was that possible? How could anyone feel their cause so strongly that they would take the life of a child to further their own agenda?

It was insane. Beyond insane.

She forced the thoughts from her mind. This bath was supposed to be about relaxing. She didn't want to think anymore. She wanted to relax and just lie here in the water and soak up the incredible heat.

Eventually she drained some of the water and used the hand-held spray attachment to wash her hair. When she'd rinsed and conditioned and felt clean and relaxed, she climbed out of the tub, drained and rinsed it, then dried her skin. She took her time and completed all the usual grooming rituals, including clipping her nails and slathering her skin with lotion. Mostly she wanted to make sure her whole body was free of any hint of the evil she'd encountered this day.

By the time she wrapped herself in her ancient terry-cloth robe and emerged from the bathroom, she felt like a new woman. She gathered her dirty clothes, opted not to try and salvage them and tossed the whole lot into the garbage. She never wanted to see those clothes again, much less wear them.

In the kitchen she considered scrounging around for something to eat, but she didn't really have an appetite. Her stomach still felt a little queasy from all the stress. Instead she poured herself a brimming stemmed glass of wine.

A couple of glasses of wine and she would feel totally relaxed. She padded into the living room and checked her machine. The red light on the message machine was flashing. Might as well see who had called. As the machine prepared to play the one message, she shuffled over to the sofa and dropped into the corner spot where she always sat.

"Miss Grant," the male voice recorded on the machine said, "this is Paul Reimes." A moment of silence passed. "I just wanted to thank you for saving my son's life. I wanted to say this in person…" His voice quavered. "But the authorities felt I should stay with my family just now, and letting you know how much I am in your debt simply wouldn't wait. Thank you. It's not nearly enough…but it's all I know to say."

Claire grabbed a tissue and swiped at her eyes. And she'd thought she was going to be able to relax. She pulled the throw up around her and grabbed the remote. Time to vegetate with a program that had nothing to do with guns or killers. She skimmed through the channels, avoiding the stations where news would be showing. She wasn't ready for that yet.

A game show captured her attention and she watched mindlessly for a while. She didn't want to think—not about anything right now.

After watching three game shows in a row her stomach started to protest the lack of attention. She kicked off the throw and moseyed into the kitchen. Another glass of wine was first on the menu. She sipped the second glass as she surveyed the contents of her fridge.

A heat-and-serve frozen dinner just wasn't going to do it tonight. She needed real sustenance. After prowling through all her usual hiding places, she found a chocolate bar and munched on it until she made a decision.

Her decision was that there simply wasn't anything in the house that spoke to her taste buds. There was only one thing to do. Call for takeout.

That was one of the things she loved about urban living. Practically every restaurant in the area would deliver. Tonight, she had Italian on her mind. A nice salad, pasta and marinara along with garlic bread. Heaven on earth.

While she waited for the food to arrive, she finished drying her tangled hair and spent what felt like forever straightening it. Her arms felt weak after so long holding up the straightening iron.

She glanced at the clock. Thirty-five minutes had passed since she'd ordered. The food should have arrived by now. Nobody got lost in Fremont. If the driver offered that excuse she might just have to skip his tip.

She scrounged in her purse for the money, then peeked out the window. There were three cars at the curb in front of her house. One, the one in the center, was marked with the name of the restaurant she'd called. The other two were generic looking sedans.

The guy in the delivery car had gotten out and stood with his hands braced on top of his car. A man behind him started to pat him down.

"What in the world?"

There were four men in all, all dressed in suits, swarming around the delivery guy.

Before her brain had time to override her reaction, she'd stalked to her front door and jerked it open. She stormed out onto the porch and yelled, "What's going on? That's my dinner he's delivering!"

Two seconds after she'd bellowed the words, she realized that only a "large" girl would go nuts when her food delivery was threatened. She rolled her eyes and wanted to kick herself. But, hey, she'd been through literal hell today. She deserved a decent meal.

Two of the men strode up the sidewalk toward her. For the first time since she'd barreled out onto her porch an inkling of uneasiness trickled through her. Maybe rushing out here hadn't been such a good idea.

"Ma'am." The first guy to reach her steps flashed a badge. "I'm going to have to ask you to step back inside the house."

She looked from him to his companion who displayed his badge as well.

"What's going on?"

"We'll explain everything, ma'am," the first guy said as he escorted her back to the door, "just as soon as you're inside."

Inside, Claire threw up her hands stop-sign fashion as the two older men came in and closed the door. "Just a minute. Why are you two here? Why are you shaking down my delivery guy?"

"Calm down, ma'am," the second guy said. "We have orders to ensure your safety."

"My safety?" She looked from one to the other. "What are you talking about?" The idea that somehow, something about today wasn't over yet nagged at her, but she refused to consider the notion. Three of the terrorists were dead. One was in custody. Everything was okay now. It had to be. She was too tired to deal with anything else.

"Ma'am, the prisoner, Bashir Rafsanjani, taken from the scene today, killed two police officers and escaped during transport. We're not exactly sure what happened. We feel you may be his next target."

"He escaped?"

You are dead!

The words echoed inside her head.

The man who had uttered them so vehemently had escaped from the police. Her brain finally wrapped around the words echoing inside her head.

He would want his revenge…on her.

Chapter 4

Tuesday morning Claire peeked beyond the blinds to see if the unmarked sedan was still parked in front of her house.

It was.

The police had stayed close by all night.

She cradled her coffee mug in hopes of warming her cold hands and did the thing she'd put off for hours now. She pressed the remote and watched as the television blinked to life.

After selecting a round-the-clock news channel, she sat back and sipped her coffee. A reporter, with Claire's school in the background, recapped the horrifying events of the day before. The escaped prisoner was still at large. Pictures of the four terrorists appeared on the screen. She peered at the image of the man she had killed. He was surely of Middle Eastern descent, yet his name was as American as her own. Thomas Odem.

Thomas Odem had been twenty-one years of age and an engineering student at Washington University. An honor student.

The warm coffee couldn't keep the iciness from sliding through her veins. If she hadn't been in the room to hear the way Odem had orchestrated the despicable act that had been carried out at her school, she would find it hard to believe he was the one. But she had been there. She'd heard him order the murder of a child. The man had been ruthless, inhuman.

And still she couldn't help feeling remorse at what fate had forced her to do.

Her mind raced back six years…to that night. Her sister had been screaming and crying, begging Claire to stop him before he hurt the baby. He'd broken in through the back door, forcing Claire and her sister to hide in the bedroom. There was no place left to run. The police had been called but they would never get there in time. One of the downfalls to country living.

Tad Farmer, her no-good brother-in-law, had

pounded and kicked until he'd succeeded in knocking in the bedroom door. The handgun he'd waved at her sister had terrified Claire. She had known this time would be different from all the others. He had beaten her sister numerous times, but this time he planned to kill her because she refused to go back to him.

When he'd rushed her sister, Claire had stepped into his path. They had struggled...somehow the weapon had gone off. Maybe he'd been trying to shoot her or maybe it had been an accident. The bullet had entered his torso at an upward angle just below his rib cage, glanced off a rib and torn straight through his heart. He'd died within two or three minutes. Claire had still been on her knees, attempting CPR on the jerk when the police stormed the house.

Her sister had gone into premature labor and had had to be rushed to the hospital.

The world changed for Claire at that moment. She'd lost everything that mattered to her.

And now she had killed again.

She pushed the memories away.

Looking back like this was a mistake. She never allowed herself to do that, she shouldn't now. It was too painful.

Sitting here watching the news was only going to encourage wallowing in self-pity. The police were outside keeping guard. She needn't worry about her safety. The best thing she could do was occupy herself with something constructive.

Claire got up and surveyed her living room. She usually waited until Saturday to clean house. Last weekend she'd planted flowers instead. Might as well get it done today. She was home. Who knew what she'd be doing on Saturday? Though she assumed Mr. Allen's memorial service would be held before then, she couldn't be sure.

After putting her cup away and shutting off the coffee machine, she pulled on a pair of sweatpants and a Seattle Seahawks T-shirt. She bunched her hair into a ponytail and gathered her cleaning supplies.

It wasn't even nine, she had the whole day ahead of her. The fact that heavy-duty housework burned some serious calories was not lost on her. Five more pounds and she would be able to get back into her favorite size-twelve regular-fit jeans without holding her breath.

Fully motivated now, she quickly laid out a strategy, then launched her attack.

By noon her little bungalow shone, from the glossy hardwood floors to the sleek tile countertops. She had to admit that the hard word had done the trick. As exhausted as she was, she felt comfortably relaxed. A quick shower and change, and she was ready to move on to papers that needed to be graded.

First, however, she needed to have lunch. She'd skipped breakfast, not on purpose but because for once she actually had no appetite. But after her rigorous cleaning frenzy she was ready to refuel.

The telephone rang as she made her way to the kitchen. She grabbed it en route. "Hello."

"Are you okay?" Darlene said, her voice frantic. "I saw the news this morning. Are the police watching your house? Oh, my God, this is terrible, Claire. I'm coming over."

In spite of the whole mess Claire had to smile. It was nice to be loved. "Yes, I'm okay. I saw the news, too, and the police are watching my house. Come over and we'll have lunch." She surveyed the offerings in her fridge. "I was about to prepare a chef salad. You know you love my salads."

Her salads included pretty much everything but the kitchen sink: pineapple and walnuts to boot.

"Sounds great," Darlene enthused, "but I'll bring my own salad dressing."

Claire harrumphed. "Fat-free doesn't mean taste-free."

"Oh, yes it does," Darlene argued. "I'll be there in fifteen."

"Be sure to identify yourself to my bodyguards otherwise you might find yourself arrested." Claire recalled the poor delivery guy last night having to endure a humiliating pat down.

"Wait, are these cops cute?"

Claire placed a bag of mixed greens on the counter. "The ones I met last night were cute, but I haven't seen the guys out there this morning up close. There was a shift change about eight."

She couldn't believe she'd had an actual shift change in police surveillance right outside her house. This kind of stuff only happened in books and movies. The whole situation felt surreal...except for the memory of yesterday's gun blast echoing in her ears. She shuddered, banished the vivid recollection.

"Okay, so make it thirty minutes," Darlene amended. "I'll need to change."

Her friend's vanity parted the dark clouds and made Claire smile again. "See you then."

She pressed the off button and left the phone on the counter as she pillaged for additional ingredients for a masterpiece salad. Darlene was thirty-five and divorced. She lamented all too often how she didn't want to be single forever. She wanted a relationship, one that would last, with a guy who appreciated her for who she was. Her determination to attain that goal was relentless.

And still Darlene was certain it wasn't going to happen in time—before she got too old to care. Claire tried to reassure her, sometimes it even worked.

Ham, cheese, tomatoes and cucumbers in her arms, she carried her bounty to the sink. She had turned thirty this year. Some part of her had acknowledged the milestone with a vague sense of failure on some fronts. She had never been married, had absolutely no prospects of a date, much less a marriage. Should she be feeling that same desperation her friend felt?

If so, she was in trouble because she didn't feel that way at all. Far from it. The idea of intimate involvement made her want to run for the hills. She hadn't had a steady boyfriend since leaving Alabama.

Pictures of her brother-in-law lying there on her bedroom floor bleeding out internally began to darken her new good mood. She switched the mental channel, refused to look. Maybe her inability to get close to anyone did spring from the events of that long-ago night. If that was the case then she was doomed because she couldn't change what she had done. And if she was honest with herself she would have to say that she would do the same thing again. In fact, she just had.

Her sister's life had been in danger. Just as Peter Reimes's life had been yesterday. She had done the only thing she could in each situation.

But somehow, deep down, that reality didn't really help.

It didn't change the fact that she had now killed two men.

Claire turned her hands palms up and stared at them.

Did that make her a different person than she had been before? She'd wondered that the first time, but the events that followed that night had evolved so quickly with such devastating results that nothing else really mattered.

She'd left her hometown after that with no idea where she would land. Months later she had been substituting at a school in Tennessee when a new friend had recommended a school from her hometown, Whitesburg Middle all the way out in one of Seattle's many suburbs. At first Claire had been reluctant to go so far, but there had been no change in her circumstances with her sister so she'd taken the leap.

That felt like a lifetime ago.

And yet, as she stared at her hands, she remembered every detail of that night she'd killed Tad as if it had only been last night.

Somehow that was where she'd failed. She'd lost her family; maybe she'd given up too easily. But she would never know now.

With monumental effort, she turned her attention to preparing the salad. Darlene would be here soon.

She washed, sliced and diced until the presentation was perfect. Lots of lovely color and texture above a bed of vibrant greens. Water or diet cola would have to do since Darlene had not yet acquired a taste for Claire's artificially sweetened iced tea.

Claire readied the table, using her best stoneware. Her only stoneware actually. She'd been hooked on the fruit motif from the moment she'd laid eyes on it. Her whole kitchen was designed around those same colors.

She checked the clock just as the doorbell rang. "Now that's perfect timing."

Having company, especially Darlene, would help to ward off memories from the past. She had enough new trouble in the present without borrowing from the past she'd worked so hard to put behind her.

She reached for the door, almost opened it, but a nagging voice reminded her to check first. She wasn't expecting anyone other than Darlene; however, there was a terrorist on the loose who might want revenge. Some part of her still found that notion completely unbelievable. But another part, a more cautious side, didn't want to take any chances.

Claire waved at Darlene, who noticed her peeking through the slats of the blind, then unlocked and opened the door.

Looking woefully depressed, Darlene sighed and announced, "Married. Both of them. Detectives Benson and Lassiter."

The cops on surveillance duty, Claire realized. She motioned for Darlene to come on inside. "Forget about that. Lunch is waiting."

Salad dressing in hand, Darlene trudged inside. "Why do all the interesting ones have to be married already? It just isn't fair."

"They might not be interesting," Claire countered. She took the bottle of dressing from her friend and led the way to the table. "Just because they're cops doesn't mean they're interesting."

"Sure it does."

The two hugged. "You holding up okay?"

Claire nodded. "I'll survive."

Darlene gave her a smile that said she didn't have a doubt.

"Sit." Claire gestured to a chair at the table. "Eating always makes me feel better." Until she had time to consider the ramifications, she thought.

"I've never dated a cop," Darlene went on as she dribbled her own fat-filled dressing on her salad. "Maybe that's where I've been going wrong."

Claire nodded and made agreeable sounds as

her friend wandered off on her tangent about the men she should have chosen. Darlene was a striking woman. Tall and slender with perfect cheekbones and amazing hazel eyes. Her long blond hair was all-natural. And she had those movie-star teeth and not a single cap or veneer. Why did a woman that gorgeous feel so panicked about her love life? It just wasn't fair.

For a few minutes they ate in silence, then Darlene started in on the whole cop theory again.

"There's that adrenaline factor," Claire reminded her. "All cops, firemen, et cetera, fall into that adrenaline-junkie zone. Their work is dangerous. Think about how unnerving it would be to have a husband who dons SWAT gear and goes into a situation like yesterday." Her gaze moved to the clock and she couldn't help thinking that the whole terrifying incident had started around this time yesterday.

"A hero," Darlene countered. "What would we do without them? Someone has to do it. A *hero*," she repeated dreamily. "I could get used to that." She blinked, looked at Claire as if she'd just remembered something vastly important. "You're an official hero, too, you know. I know you didn't watch, but you were all over the news last night. The whole country now knows that you single-handedly saved those children."

"I didn't single-handedly do anything." Claire stood. "I think it's time for dessert." She shook her head at her friend's plunge into the twilight zone. "Something thick and chocolatey to bring you back to your senses."

She had just the stuff. It hadn't come from a bakery or a fancy shop with a dessert chef. Nope, her chocolate mousse came in a pack of four small containers from a supermarket. If you spooned it into stemmed glasses, added a dollop of whipped topping and sprinkled it with her secret ingredient, powdered chocolate sugar, it was almost impossible to tell the difference.

Any good Southern girl who didn't know how to bake quickly learned how to fudge it. Another thing all good Southern girls knew was that you didn't take credit for a blessing straight from God. The fact that she and the children had survived yesterday was nothing less than exactly that kind of blessing.

When the dessert looked restaurant-presentable, Claire waltzed back into the dining room and announced, "Viola!"

"You shouldn't have gone to so much trouble." Darlene reached for her dessert.

"It was nothing," Claire quipped.

Her depressed friend popped a spoonful into her mouth. "Mmm. Yummy."

There was no more talk of good-looking cops or love lives or lack thereof. Chocolate could always be counted on to soothe the wicked beast whether depression, envy or just plain old impatience.

Claire went all out. Even served coffee in the living room after dessert. It was that kind of day. One where she felt the need to celebrate the things she was lucky to have: good friends, a great job, nice home, food to eat, gourmet ground roast. All the necessities of life.

"Oh, I meant to tell you." Darlene sat her half-empty cup on the table next to the sofa. "Mr. Allen's service will be tomorrow. The school board is working with the family to make this a community-wide service."

"I'm glad." Claire put her cup aside, feeling warm and satisfied. "The entire community should come out and show their support and respect for Mr. Allen and his family. I'm going to miss him."

"The whole school is going to miss him." Darlene tucked her feet under her and got more comfortable. She had claimed one end of the sofa while Claire curled up on the other. "Speaking of school, there won't be any tomorrow either. We'll resume classes on Thursday. When I talked to Peg, I asked her about your classroom and she said you would be using the small auditorium for a while."

Peg Mason was Mr. Allen's secretary. "That'll

work." Claire hadn't really thought about where she would teach her class when school resumed. She hadn't thought about much the last twenty-four hours...other than the past and the horrific moments in her classroom yesterday.

"You could take a few more days off if you feel the need," Darlene suggested.

"No." Claire shook her head adamantly. "I couldn't do that to my students. They're going to need familiarity. Consistency will be very important in moving beyond this trauma."

"You're right." Darlene reached for her coffee and, as if she could sense Claire drifting back into troubling waters, she said, "So, have you ever dated a cop?"

Claire had to laugh. The woman was like a dog with a bone. "I can try and set you up if you're that interested."

Her friend chewed her lip for a moment. "Do you know how long they'll need to keep an eye on you? I mean, have you heard whether or not they've caught the guy?"

You are dead!

Claire blinked away the ugly words reverberating in her head. "Nothing. They haven't told me anything." She lifted one shoulder in a half-hearted shrug. "But then I haven't asked any questions. I suppose I should."

Darlene patted her hand. "It's only been twenty-four hours. Give yourself a little time. Surely someone will bring you up to speed by this evening or tomorrow morning at the latest. They can't expect you to stay shut up in here forever."

"I should hope not."

The telephone rang. Claire started at the unexpected sound. She pressed her hand to her chest. "I've got to get past being so jumpy."

"You want me to get it?" Darlene was already getting up.

"Sure." Claire dropped her feet to the floor, but didn't bother getting up. "Thanks."

"Hello."

Claire twisted in her seat and parted the blind slats on the window behind her sofa. The dark sedan still sat across the street. Should she go out there and offer the officers something to eat or drink? Coffee?

Behind her, she heard Darlene ask, "Who's calling?"

Did cops on a stakeout order from a restaurant that delivered or did they bring a sack lunch? Okay, her thoughts were really drifting here.

"Claire."

She turned away from the window. Darlene offered her the receiver. Keeping her voice down so the caller wouldn't hear, Claire asked, "Who is it?"

Darlene raised her shoulders up then let them fall. "He didn't give his name, just said he was from the Homicide Division."

Could be Detective Atwood. "Thanks." Claire accepted the receiver. "Hello."

"Is this Claire Grant, the teacher from Whitesburg Middle School?"

Definitely not Atwood. The voice was deeper, more stilted. "Yes, it is. Who is this?" Maybe not stilted, maybe a slight European accent.

"I am Abdul Nusair."

Her mouth dropped open but failed to form the words of denial that burned in her brain. Her heart started to thunder, making the blood roar in her ears.

"Claire Grant, you will die for your transgression. *Over and over again.*"

A click signaled the call was over.

Claire stared at the receiver, uncertain she had heard what she thought she'd heard.

"Who was that?"

Claire looked from the phone to her friend. "Abdul Nusair."

A mixture of disbelief and fear claimed Darlene's expression. "What?"

Claire licked her lips and sucked in a sudden breath. "He said I was going to die...over and over again."

Chapter 5

There was a sudden pounding at the front door. Claire wheeled around to face the possible threat.

"Call 911, Claire!"

But the police were right outside...weren't they?

Darlene snatched the phone out of her hand and entered the three digits.

"Miss Grant, this is Detective Atwood, please open the door."

Claire held up a hand for Darlene to wait a second. "I recognize the voice. It's the detective who was at the school yesterday."

"I'm sorry, it's okay now," Darlene said to the 911 operator. "The police are already here."

Leaving her friend to explain the situation to the 911 operator, Claire started to unlock the door but hesitated. She did recognize the voice but she needed to be sure. She peeked out the window and confirmed that it was indeed the detective from yesterday. He was alone.

She gave the dead bolt a twist and opened the door. "Detective Atwood—"

"Miss Grant," he cut her off before she could ask any questions, "you're going to have to come with me."

Perspiration had beaded on the man's forehead and his face was red as if he'd run around the block a couple of times in his nice suit. She glanced out at the sedan still parked at the curb on her side of the street. The two officers inside were staring back at her. But Atwood hadn't been with them. Where was his car?

"What's going on, Detective?"

"I'm sorry, ma'am, but there's no time to explain." He reached for her arm to usher her out the door. "You should come with me *now.*"

"Wait just a minute." Darlene stepped in front of Claire. "Where are you taking her and why?"

Atwood craned his neck to check the street and yard. "Please. There is no time. We have to go. *Now!*"

Darlene turned to Claire. "I wouldn't—"

Before she could say anything else, the detective grabbed Darlene's arm and pulled her around to face him. "Unless you want to be placed under arrest for obstructing an officer of the law, I would suggest you move out of the way, ma'am." As if realizing his tactics might come across as somewhat more than pushy, he explained, more calmly, "Please, ma'am, this is an urgent situation."

"It's okay, Darlene." Claire stepped around her and out onto the porch. "I'll be fine."

Darlene glared at the detective. "She's not going anywhere without me."

"Fine." Atwood turned to Claire. "You might want to get your purse, Miss Grant. You'll want to lock up as well."

Claire went back inside and got her purse and, noticing her friend's, grabbed Darlene's. As she exited this time, she locked the door behind her.

She didn't miss the way Detective Atwood kept surveying the area as he escorted her and Darlene to the street. Claire had been certain he would guide them to the sedan, but he didn't. She saw the front end of another vehicle parked around the north corner of the intersection just past her house. Maybe that was Atwood's car. Just how many cops did they have watching her?

A black SUV rolled up in front of the sidewalk where they had come to a stop.

Claire and Darlene exchanged a look of uneasiness.

What was happening here?

Atwood opened the rear passenger's door of the SUV and waited for the two of them to climb in.

"It's all right, ladies," he explained. "We're taking you to a safe place."

Claire met Darlene's worried gaze again. What else could they do? She could ask questions but Atwood's sense of urgency was palpable. If you didn't trust the police, who did you trust?

A man claiming to be the most feared terrorist on the planet had just called Claire's home and threatened her. Obviously she couldn't stay here. How could a sedan with two officers on surveillance duty stop a terrorist at the very pinnacle of the top ten list?

Claire gazed back at her home one last time.

"Please, ma'am," Atwood urged, "we have to go now."

Claire climbed into the SUV, Darlene scooted in beside her. Atwood closed the door and the vehicle rolled forward, gaining speed as they left her neighborhood behind.

Claire dragged the seat belt across her lap and watched her friend do the same. The two men in the front seat scarcely acknowledged their presence. The driver had glanced back via the rearview mirror as Claire had gotten in but the dark sunglasses he wore prevented her from seeing his eyes.

Claire took Darlene's hand and held it tightly. She had never appreciated her friend more than she did at this moment. It took guts to go blindly into the unknown for a friend.

Funny, Claire realized, her own sister, a woman who shared her DNA, hadn't been willing to stand by her like that six years ago...not even after Claire had saved her life as well as her unborn child's.

The driver took a number of unexpected turns and strange detours. Either he wasn't familiar with downtown Seattle or he had purposely chosen a zigzagging, backtracking route to his destination.

Soon they were closing in on the Plaza, the most luxurious hotel in the city. Unbelievably, the swanky place seemed to be their destination.

The driver rolled up to the lavish entrance and shifted into Park. He and the front-seat passenger immediately emerged from the vehicle, took a long look around, then opened the rear doors for Claire and Darlene. The second man wore those same dark glasses, making reading his intent virtually impossible. Both men wore suits and ties just as Detective Atwood had, except these ensembles appeared considerably more expensive. Not the off-the-rack jobs from the mall or the less-exclusive department stores.

Another man in a similar suit, sans the sunglasses, showed up, took the keys and climbed into the SUV. Claire and Darlene were guided into the vast lobby by the same two gentlemen who'd brought them here. Very strange.

Gleaming marble and copious amounts of flowers greeted their arrival. The distinguished lobby left no doubt as to the grandeur of the accommodations. Claire might actually have felt like a celebrity with an entourage if she hadn't caught a glimpse of one of the men's shoulder holster beneath his elegant jacket.

"This way, ladies."

Startled, Claire stared at the man who had driven the SUV. It was the first time either of the men had spoken. His voice was deep and unsettling somehow. She wanted to ask questions, but she couldn't seem to find her own voice. She should ask questions, but she couldn't bring herself to string the words together much less utter anything sensible.

Besides, as long as she didn't know the real story, she could pretend anything.

When they boarded the glamorous elevator, Claire thought of the movies and television shows she'd seen where witnesses were taken into protective custody. Not once had she seen a single one provided with accommodations quite this opulent. But then, why else would she and Darlene be brought to a hotel? Atwood had said they were being taken to a safe place. This must be it.

If Nusair had located her telephone number, which wouldn't have been a problem for him or anyone else since she was listed in the telephone directory, it was a given that he would just as easily find her home.

Did this mean she couldn't go back home until Nusair was captured?

That could be…*never.*

What about her job…her meticulously planted flowers…her new, carefully constructed life?

The elevator stopped on the fourteenth floor.

One of their escorts stepped out of the car and waited for Claire and Darlene to do the same. Strangely, the other man remained on the elevator.

Their guide led them to room 1427. He knocked and a few seconds later the door opened. He motioned for Claire and Darlene to precede him into the room.

Once they were inside, the door closed and the lock was engaged. Claire turned back to the door but the man who had driven them to this location had not come into the room behind them.

Her pulse hitched. What was going on here? This was all entirely too clandestine for comfort.

"Miss Grant, you and Miss Vernon should make yourselves comfortable."

Claire looked from Darlene to the man who'd spoken. Another suit and tie, same expensive taste. He gestured to the sitting area near what was likely a wall of windows overlooking greater Seattle, but the heavy drapes were drawn closed.

Grabbing her friend by the arm, Claire led the way. When they'd taken seats and the man who'd asked them to do so had moved into one of the adjoining rooms, Claire leaned close to Darlene. "Who do you think these people are? More cops?"

"I don't know. FBI maybe?"

Claire glanced around the room. A door on each side led to what she presumed to be bedrooms. A two-bedroom suite possibly. The generous seating arrangement was part of a parlor that consisted of an area with a round table and six chairs, a desk, a small fridge and a sink. The handsomely upholstered furnishings were elegant, the decor richly appointed.

Not exactly your typical hotel room.

If she listened carefully she could hear low voices in the room to her left. Three or more people, she decided after eavesdropping for several more moments. A meeting or conference call.

The man who'd directed them to be seated entered the room once more. "Miss Grant, I'll need you to come with me, please."

Her pulse racing, Claire stood. Darlene did the same.

"Miss Vernon, I'll have to ask you to remain here until Miss Grant has completed her briefing."

Darlene started to argue but Claire stopped her. "It's okay. I'll be fine." A briefing she could handle. A briefing meant information. She needed information. She wanted to know what the heck was going on.

Darlene didn't like it, but she relented.

Claire turned to the man who'd given the orders and took a deep breath.

With a hand at her elbow, he steered her into the adjoining room on the right. To Claire's surprise what should have been a bedroom had been transformed into a conference room. A long mahogany table with royal-blue upholstered chairs lining all sides dominated the center of the space. Against the wall were credenza-type tables with everything from copiers and fax machines to stacks of files and other office equipment not readily identifiable but ready for use.

"Have a seat, Miss Grant, the team will be with you in a moment."

The team? She pivoted to ask what that meant but the man who'd ushered her into the room walked out before she could manage the question, pulling the double doors closed as he went.

Sitting wasn't an option. She wanted to know

why she was here and who these people were. FBI? Homeland Security? Maybe CIA. Who knew?

Claire walked straight over to the stacks of files and surveyed the mounds of paperwork and the gray folders. Her breath caught in her throat as she recognized the Federal Bureau of Investigation emblem on the letterhead of one page.

It was the FBI. Darlene had guessed right.

Made sense, she supposed. But why did they want to talk to her here?

They could have questioned her at the police precinct or the bureau field office.

Why the elaborate setup? The secretiveness?

Claire Grant, you will die for your transgression. Over and over again.

A chill ran through her, making her wish she'd grabbed a jacket. This was about him. The idea that she had been ushered over here immediately after that call couldn't be coincidence.

Even she wasn't that naive.

Did that mean…?

The doors flew open drawing her attention to the other side of the room.

A man, another she hadn't seen before, followed by an entourage, strode purposefully toward her. The leader of the group wore the same uniform as the others, suit and tie. He was tall, broad shouldered and carried himself with an air of importance.

He had the most unusual green eyes. It was impossible not to notice. Classic good looks and that air of importance one saw in high-profile politicians.

"Miss Grant, I'm Special Agent in Charge Luke Krueger." He indicated the long mahogany table with a sweep of his right hand. "Please join me at the conference table."

The man's deep, authoritative tone made Claire uneasy somehow, but she pulled out the closest chair and sat down. Cooperation was likely the key to learning as much information as possible.

Krueger strode to the opposite end of the table and waited until his colleagues had settled in. Four men and one woman. She didn't recognize any of them from the scene at the school yesterday. Krueger stood at the head of the table, a statement of his position. Claire chose a seat at the end farthest from him and with two chairs separating her from the next nearest agent. That was perfectly fine by her.

The man who had brought her to the room appeared and passed out a bound report of some sort to everyone seated, including Claire. He then assumed a position at the door as if guarding it to ensure no one else entered. She didn't open the report since no one else at the table bothered.

She wondered if Darlene were alone in the parlor now or if one of the other men they'd met on the journey over here had arrived to keep her company. Darlene would definitely like that.

"Miss Grant, if I may have your full attention."

Embarrassed that she'd been caught with her mind elsewhere, Claire shifted her gaze to Krueger, who remained standing.

He stared directly at her with an unsettling intensity. Those extraordinary green eyes seemed to bore right through her but she didn't look away. She couldn't have at this point, even if she'd wanted to.

"To my left," he said as he gestured to the woman sitting on Claire's side of the table, "is Special Agent Betty Nance. Next to her are Special Agents Craig Carver and Skyler Goldbach."

Claire looked from one agent to the next, presented the best smile she had to offer under the circumstances. Some part of her wondered if a mistake had been made. Why would the FBI invite her to a briefing?

"On my right are Special Agents Ronald Maxwell and Andy Talkington. That's Special Agent Todd Holman at the door."

She managed an acknowledging nod as she surveyed the group, wondered again what in the world she was doing with this room full of federal agents.

"Today," Krueger said, drawing her gaze as well

as her attention back to him, "at 2:04 p.m., you received a telephone call from Abdul Nusair."

She blinked, startled or maybe unsettled. The FBI had been monitoring her calls?

"That's right." She moistened her lips. Everyone at the table was staring at her now.

"What do you know about Nusair?"

Krueger took off his jacket and hung it over the back of the chair in front of him. Her gaze followed the movement, noting the graceful action with maybe a little too much interest. She was going to have to stop letting Darlene's desperation for a relationship rub off on her. Fixating on a stranger's physical assets wasn't her usual style.

"Nothing," she admitted in answer to his question. She chewed her lip as she considered what Darlene had told her. "Well, I mean, I've heard the name on the news." She cleared her throat softly in a futile attempt to give her brain time to string together the proper response. "He's a terrorist."

Krueger pulled out the chair and lowered his tall frame into it with that same undeniable grace. "That's correct."

Claire felt like a student the teacher had singled out for humiliation. No one had made her feel this on the spot since college.

Krueger leaned back in his chair and stared at her as if waiting for additional details. She didn't really have much more to give him but something was better than nothing she supposed.

"My friend said he's on some sort of top ten list." Wait, that wasn't right. That was the other terrorist she'd told her about. "Nusair is the…ah… most evil terrorist in the world. I suppose he's at the very top of that list."

Krueger loosened his tie. He had long fingers. Broad shoulders, too, she realized as her gaze traced the path from the tie he'd loosened to the tested seams of the crisp white shirt outlining those wide shoulders. Wait, she'd already noticed the shoulders. Stop it, she told herself again.

"Abdul Nusair," Krueger went on where she'd left off, "rose up from a well-known terrorist group with cells in a number of Middle Eastern countries, including Israel, most major European capitals and far too many cities to name here in the States. He specializes in blowing things up. He made a name for himself rather swiftly, became the new leader to watch, as we say in the Bureau."

If she was supposed to comment on that information she had no idea what to say, other than her first thought of *Dear God*. She was reasonably sure that the depth of her dismay would not impress these people.

"As you suggested, Nusair is at the very top of

our wanted list. Our agency, as well as the CIA, has focused unparalleled effort on trying to capture him, dead or alive."

He paused, apparently to permit that statement to penetrate fully.

Claire worked hard to maintain eye contact. She didn't generally have this much trouble doing so but Krueger made her tremendously uncomfortable. Nervous to the point of needing to fidget. Incredibly, she kept her hands at rest and tucked away in her lap.

"That effort has failed to this point. Nusair is not only a highly intelligent adversary, he is fiercely cunning and utterly ruthless. He prefers to manipulate his army of devoted followers rather than risk personal involvement in his schemes. His followers look up to him in a way not unlike Christians do Jesus Christ himself."

Just when Claire thought nothing he could say would shock her, those words did. The idea that there were people out there who believed in a mere man to the point that they would kill masses of innocent people made her sick to her stomach.

"Nusair has claimed credit for the recent bombings in London where upwards of one hundred civilians lost their lives. Last year his followers bombed a dozen nightclubs in Europe, claiming that the clubs promoted American music and, therefore, embraced American ways." Krueger pushed away the report lying on the table before him, not bothering to open it. "I could go on and on, Miss Grant. Nusair is responsible for thousands of wrongful deaths. He is pure evil and no one seems to be able to stop him since he never does his own dirty work. He stays in hiding and masterminds his monstrous plots."

All eyes were on Claire then.

Was she supposed to say something now?

"The man who died as a result of your intervention in yesterday's kidnapping attempt," Krueger said, drawing her attention back to him, "lived here in Seattle under an alias."

Thomas Odem. The name reverberated through her. She found it almost humorous the way Krueger danced all around the fact that she had *killed* Odem. She couldn't be sure if he was being kind or was simply leading up to something and didn't want her on the defensive.

He needn't have worried. She was all too aware of what she had done in that classroom yesterday. Forgetting wasn't likely.

Krueger went on, "One year ago Odem transferred to Washington University from an engineering institute in Toronto. We've been watching him since. To date, more than a dozen suspected followers of Nusair have converged upon Seattle.

Similar cells have formed in Los Angeles and San Francisco, as well as three southern cities and four more along the east coast. In each case, most of the cell members are enrolled in local universities and appear to be quiet, honor-roll students."

Again Krueger's silence sat heavily on her shoulders.

"The man involved in the horrific events at my school yesterday, the one who escaped, Bashir Rafsanjani, was a part of the cell here in Seattle?" She knew he was, but she had to say something. She needed to know where this was going and how it involved her. Every instinct told her that Krueger was going some place specific with this history lesson.

"That's correct. Rafsanjani was a student at Washington University, as were the other two men involved in yesterday's attack."

Students. Unbelievable.

Claire abruptly remembered the other element in the equation—how the men who attacked her classroom were trying to gain freedom for their colleague.

"How is Hamid Kaibar connected to all this?"

Krueger and the agent sitting to his immediate right shared a look that set her on edge…further on edge than she already was.

"Hamid Kaibar," Krueger began, "is our number-two dirtbag on that list you mentioned. Catching him was a major coup."

"Is he cooperating? Kaibar, I mean."

"Not yet."

Another of those covert looks between the two men. This was really making her nervous.

"Yesterday was about getting Kaibar freed," she said, deciding to fish for more information. "Does your agency believe that this group—this cell—has some major terrorist event planned for Seattle?"

Krueger didn't answer her right away, but that relentless gaze continued to drill right through her. She began tapping her right foot nervously beneath the table.

"Miss Grant, we believe that Nusair is in the process of orchestrating a major event in nearly a dozen cities across our country. The Seattle cell, in our estimation, is the final positioning in preparation for that multicity event."

Fear sank its sharp talons deep into her chest. She knew what this meant…possibly something far worse than the catastrophe on September 11, 2001.

She stared at the official emblem on the report in front of her. Then she squeezed her eyes shut. She didn't want to know about this.

How could she go on with her life now, pretending that the threat wasn't there? Now she knew firsthand these sorts of radical extremists were never going to stop.

That tragic September day not so many years ago had only been the beginning.

She lifted her gaze back to Krueger. He, like the others around the table, waited patiently for her to make the next move. She had no idea what they wanted from her. "Why are you telling me this?" Maybe the question sounded selfish or cowardly, but she was only a teacher. What did she have to offer that would help in a national security crisis?

"Miss Grant," Krueger said, his voice lower, softer now, "we have utilized every asset at our disposal and we have not been able even to get close to Abdul Nusair. *Until now.*"

Claire realized that the other shoe was about to drop.

"As I told you before, Thomas Odem was an alias. We ascertained the man's identity several months ago and that caused us to focus our investigation on Seattle. The Seattle cell is the primary cell," he explained. "Whatever is planned for Seattle is the key, the catalyst, so to speak, of Nusair's ultimate plan. We are absolutely certain about that."

Now she started to see the big picture. Odem, or whoever he was, had been the FBI's prime suspect. The most pivotal part of their investigation.

And she had killed him.

Renewed dread congealed in her belly.

"Thomas Odem," Krueger said somberly, "was born Habib Nusair."

Claire frowned. The full implications of this statement hit her as Krueger continued.

"Habib was Abdul Nusair's only son."

Chapter 6

"Miss Grant and I will need a few moments alone."

The people in the room rose from their chairs and filed out, each stealing a last fleeting look at Claire as they passed.

She told herself to breathe deeply, to focus on slowing the runaway pounding in her chest. Hands clasped tightly in her lap, she stared at the unopened report in front of her as if it might reveal the answers she needed. A part of her just couldn't evaluate Krueger's revelation all at once even though she had connected the dots mere seconds before his confirmation. She had to take it one facet at a time.

Habib Nusair, the man she'd killed, was the only son of Abdul Nusair, the single most vicious terrorist on the planet.

She swallowed hard, let that knowledge absorb fully.

Abdul would want his revenge.

On her.

…you will die for your transgression.

"We have a very sensitive situation, Miss Grant."

She looked up at the man, Special Agent in Charge Luke Krueger. It was only the two of them now. The others most likely waited in the parlor with Darlene.

He hadn't asked his team to leave for no reason. He had something on his mind. Something he wanted to discuss with her in private.

Since she couldn't read minds, she opted for her own line of questioning. "Am I in protective custody, Agent Krueger?"

Those extraordinary green eyes peered fully into hers, making her want to widen the distance between them. There was something about his eyes that made her restless or uncertain of herself.

"Yes, you are."

Okay. Deep breath. "The FBI has been monitoring my calls?" That was fairly obvious, but she needed an explanation. A confirmation of her assumptions actually. She had some ideas about that, but she wanted it straight from the source.

Krueger got up from his chair and walked around to where she sat. He pulled out the chair next to her and settled into it. This close her senses picked up on the subtle hint of fruity aftershave, something fresh and natural, he wore.

He turned slightly in his chair so that he could face her more fully. Her pulse stumbled erratically making her feel totally foolish.

"Miss Grant, the moment Habib Nusair's body was identified, the Bureau started monitoring everything about you." He propped one elbow on the table and the other on the back of his chair. "By the time my flight from Reagan National arrived at Sea-Tac International, I already knew what flavor of ice cream you prefer."

If his intent was to intimidate, he had succeeded on a grand scale.

"Why would you need to know so much about me?" The idea that he knew about her past, all of it, made her want to squirm, but she wouldn't. She was one of the victims here. She wasn't the bad guy.

This close she could see the darker, almost black, inner circles around his irises. The slightest crinkling around his eyes suggested he'd likely seen the last of his early thirties. Thirty-five or -six perhaps. That he was incredibly charismatic made bad matters way worse. She didn't want to notice any of this.

This was not the time to be needy and hopeful.

"Whether you know it or not," Krueger said, his voice low and quiet, lacking the intimidation factor this time, "Miss Grant, you are now the linchpin of our ongoing investigation. For all intents and purposes you're our ace in the hole."

How could she be a key player in this? If anything she was a target for terrorists. Her stock quotient had bottomed out in any trading market other than one that was very black and very lethal.

"I don't know anything, Agent Krueger. The terrorists didn't say anything during the time they held us in that classroom. As much as I'd like to, how could I possibly help your investigation?"

For three or four frantic beats of her heart he studied her, looked so deeply into her eyes she could scarcely breathe. Why did he do that?

"Abdul Nusair had only one son."

Yes, they had established that fact already. She didn't say as much since she didn't want to antagonize the man.

"Nusair isn't a young man. He fathered a half dozen daughters before getting the son he wanted. He's well into his sixties now. He had high hopes for his son. Hopes that included his carrying their cause into the next generation. This loss is probably the one tragedy that could truly devastate the man."

As it would any father. But this wasn't just any father, this was a ruthless terrorist.

"In all the years that I've been tracking Nusair, we've never been this close to him. Habib's presence here in Seattle was the opportunity we'd been waiting for. Nusair kept his son underground until recently. Discovering him here was a huge break. It's also an indication of how short our time is. Plans have clearly escalated. Habib was put in place for a reason."

"And I killed him," Claire cut to the chase. "I've ruined your investigation. Any hope you had of capturing Nusair died with his son yesterday." She'd foiled a high-priority investigation involving national security. Talk about making her mark in history.

"Not necessarily," Krueger countered.

It was official, she was thoroughly confused now.

"The fact is," he went on, "your heroic measure may have provided us with our first real opportunity to take him down."

She searched his eyes. Tried to read what he wasn't telling her. "You're going to have to explain what you mean, Agent Krueger."

"Abdul Nusair won't stop until he has avenged

his son's death. No matter how long it takes, he will kill you or die trying."

She went ice cold. "Is that why I'm in protective custody?" That seemed like the logical explanation, but some part of her understood that there was more…far more.

"In part."

He sat back, distanced himself. It was more than his physical movement. She felt his withdrawal as literally as she saw it.

"We need you, Miss Grant. If we don't stop Nusair while we're this close we won't ever have this opportunity again. We have every reason to believe his cells are poised to make a catastrophic move. Stopping Nusair is essential."

"You're not afraid that his minions will carry on without him?" Even if they stopped Nusair there was no guarantee his people would walk away from whatever schemes he had orchestrated.

"We have his right-hand man, Hamid Kaibar. I'm certain his continued silence hinges upon Nusair. Once Nusair is out of the way, we'll get everything we need from Kaibar."

That left the pivotal question of how they intended to get Nusair in the first place. Somehow the answer to that question involved her. She was beginning to understand what Krueger had in mind for her.

"So," she ventured, "I'm the bait."

The idea hadn't felt real until she said the words out loud.

It was true. She saw the confirmation in his eyes before he blinked it away.

"*Bait* isn't the word I would use."

Now that intense gaze found someplace else to land. Anyplace but on her it seemed.

"What word would you use?" The cold hard reality of her fate had begun to sink in fully, kindling a survival reaction, however delayed. It wasn't that she didn't want to help make her country a safe place. On the contrary, she did. It was the idea that this man and his team only saw her as one thing, a means to an end. That part made her furious.

"You're an asset, Miss Grant. The security of your country may very well depend on you."

The cold fear that had invaded her body from the moment she'd received that threatening call had given way to numbness. Along the way she'd felt anticipation, frustration and even irritation. But this feeling was beyond all that.

Maybe it was resignation. Yes, that was it. She now realized the full ramifications of her predicament.

She was a dead woman…anyway you looked at it.

Either Nusair would kill her or the FBI would get her killed attempting to lure him in.

"I know this isn't exactly an optimal position, Miss Grant. Let me assure you that your safety will be paramount throughout this operation."

That promise prompted a dry laugh from her throat. She hadn't meant to let it escape. *Optimal*—definitely not. "I thought stopping Nusair was paramount, Agent Krueger."

His guard went up. She noted the change in his expression as surely as she felt the disruption in her own heart's rhythm at the idea that her options were limited. No matter the outcome of this conversation, she had little choice in what happened next.

"Do you have a problem making certain sacrifices for your country, Miss Grant?"

Fury ignited in her belly. That he tacked her name onto practically every statement he made was nothing more than a way to keep her off guard…feeling inferior somehow.

"Of course not. It's just that I'm a little surprised at your sidestepping the real issue here."

"And what is the real issue from your perspective?"

"This operation will most likely get me killed. Ensuring my safety will only be a priority as long as it doesn't interfere with getting Nusair. I know that. You know that. I just want to hear you say it."

The standoff lasted all of ten seconds.

Claire couldn't say for sure exactly why it was

so important to her for this man to admit his real intent, but somehow it was.

"Your safety is and will be priority one."

For another beat or two she was certain he intended to leave it at that…a lie.

"But if a choice has to be made, completing the ultimate goal will take precedence. You surely see there is no other way," Krueger continued.

Well, at least he was honest.

"That's all I needed to hear."

Claire stood.

His gaze remained fixed on hers.

"I need to talk to my friend before…" How did she phrase this? "…before we go any further."

"Of course." He pushed back his chair and rose to his full, confidence-stealing height. "I'll send her in so that the two of you will have some privacy."

Special Agent Luke Krueger walked out of the room.

Claire closed her eyes to hold back the emotion brimming there and steadied herself. Promised herself she would not cry. She would not take this like a sissy. Her father had raised her to be stronger than this.

"Claire."

She blinked rapidly and rearranged her expression into one of optimism before turning to greet her best friend. "Hey."

Scanning the unexpected furnishings in the room, Darlene hurried over to where Claire waited.

"What's going on here?"

"You were right," Claire told her. "These guys are FBI. That call I received really was from Abdul Nusair. Apparently he's decided to make me pay for protecting my students." She couldn't bring herself to say "for killing his son," out loud.

Darlene seemed to digest that information for a moment. "Was the man you had to kill yesterday important to him?" She flashed her palms in a gesture of doubt. "I mean, beyond being one of his overzealous, fruitcake followers?"

Claire braced herself for saying what she should have known she couldn't keep from her friend. "The man I killed was his son." She held Darlene's gaze a moment. "His only son."

Darlene reached for her, took her hands. "Oh, God, Claire. What're they going to do to protect you?"

Her eyes started to burn again. She blinked, fighting the overwhelming urge to break down and cry. "They're going to do all they can." She glanced toward the door. "I don't have a lot of time, but I wanted to talk to you before I have to go wherever they're planning to take me next."

Darlene squeezed her hands. "This is crazy. There has to be something they can do."

Claire shook her head. She appreciated that her friend cared so much, but she was wrong. There was nothing anyone could do. "I won't be able to attend Mr. Allen's memorial service. I'd like you to let Mrs. Allen know how deeply sorry I am. Please tell her that her husband gave his life to protect the children." She had to stop a moment to compose herself.

Darlene waited patiently for her to continue.

"I'll need to be put on extended leave. I don't know when I'll be able to come back."

Tears started to roll down Darlene's cheeks, but, to her credit, she remained stoically silent.

"Take care of my place for me. You know where I keep the spare key hidden. If you let my flowers die I'll be seriously unhappy."

Darlene laughed, the sound sort of pitiful. "You know I will."

Claire nodded. "I know I can count on you." She inhaled a deep, bolstering breath. This was where things got tricky. "In my bedroom, under the mattress, there's a diary I keep."

"A diary?" Darlene's watery eyes went wide with glee. "You shouldn't have told me about that. You know I'll have to read it."

Claire bit down on her lower lip when it trembled. Don't lose it yet, she ordered. "The… ah…diary is for my sister."

All signs of amusement vanished from her friend's face. "I didn't know you had a sister."

"We don't exactly keep in touch. Just make sure she gets the diary if…things…well, you know if they stick me in some witness protection program where I can't contact anyone in my former life." She pushed a smile into place. "That happens all the time in the movies. Her name and address is inside the front cover."

"What is it you're not telling me?"

Darlene stared at Claire, her suspicion mounting.

"Don't be paranoid." Claire laughed, a painful sound not much better than the one Darlene had made moments ago. "You know me, I'm just covering all my bases. You know how anal I am."

Darlene still wasn't convinced. Claire could see the questions in her eyes.

"Don't lie to me, Claire. What's really going on?"

"Miss Grant. Miss Vernon."

Claire tensed as Agent Krueger entered the room. She'd known he would be listening. That whole line of bull about the privacy had been just that, bull. Either that or the man had damned good timing.

"I apologize, Miss Vernon, but we're going to have to be going now. Agents Nance and Goldbach will take you home."

"Where is Claire going?" Darlene demanded, staring straight into those intense green eyes. "I want your assurance that she's going to be well protected."

Agent Krueger gestured to the door. "You have my word, Miss Vernon. Now, the agents are waiting to take you home."

Darlene hugged her. Claire held on tight, didn't want to let go but she knew Krueger was waiting.

The tearful goodbye tore a chunk out of Claire's heart. She watched her friend go, scared to death she would never see her again.

She turned back to Krueger. "How can you be sure Darlene will be safe? If Nusair knows she's my friend he might—"

"Already taken care of. Two agents will be watching her every move, twenty-four/seven."

A sigh of relief expelled from her lungs. Wait. What about her sister?

"I have a sister and a niece." God, she should have thought of that sooner. Nusair could already be trying to get to them.

"Agents have already been dispatched to watch your sister. For now we're doing so without briefing her as to the situation." Krueger touched her arm in an attempt at reassurance. "We don't leave anything to chance, Miss Grant. The people you care about will be protected."

His hand felt warm against her skin. She wanted to believe what he said…that nothing would be left to chance. But she was afraid. Afraid for the only family she had left, whether that family claimed her or not. Afraid for her dear friend.

"What do we do now?" She felt suddenly tired. as if the weight of the world were on her shoulders and she had no idea how to support it properly.

"I'll need a list of the items you require from your home." He moved those broad shoulders in a negligible shrug. "Clothes, toiletries, any medications. Then we'll start the operation briefing."

Krueger rounded up a notepad and a pen and placed both on the table. "Let me know when you're finished and I'll send one of my agents to pick up your stuff."

Claire sat down at the conference table once more and stared at the paper. She tried to look at the chore before her as if she were taking a vacation. A couple of weeks in the mountains or on a cruise, though she wouldn't need any formal attire for sure.

Unless she wanted to go ahead and pick out a dress to be buried in.

A shiver rushed over her skin.

She couldn't start thinking that way. Krueger said he would do all he could to protect her. She had to do her part as well. If she fell into the role of victim, she'd certainly end up a victim. She had to be strong and think rationally. She was no shrinking violet. She knew how to use a handgun, a rifle and she knew how to fight. Sisters as close in age as she and her sister didn't grow up without a scuffle or two.

Claire started with clothes. Moved on to toiletries, only the necessities. Maybe the iron she used for straightening her hair wasn't an actual necessity but maintaining some aspects of her appearance would help her keep her composure. Her hair was one of them.

At first she left off the box of exquisite chocolates she had saved for a special occasion but then she decided that she needed it.

An epiphany struck just then.

This was almost like being pregnant.

Her friends always told her that the great thing about being pregnant was the fact that a woman didn't have to worry about watching her food intake so closely. Unless there were complications, dieting was a no-no during pregnancy.

The way Claire saw it, her current circumstances were quite similar. Why fret about what she ate? She might not live to ever have to worry about climbing onto a scale again.

There you go. Her mother had always taught her to look at the bright side of any situation.

Claire had just proven that almost any situation could have a lighter side. Who cared about her weight if the size of the casket were the only issue?

She'd really gone off the deep end here. After reviewing her list she decided she couldn't think of anything else. As if he'd sensed her completion of the task, Krueger returned.

Maybe they had cameras as well as listening devices monitoring this room.

She got up and passed the list to him.

He scanned it, then settled his full attention on her. "If you think of anything else you need, just let me know. We want you to be comfortable."

Agent Carver rushed into the room. "Excuse me, sir."

Krueger shifted his attention to the other agent. "What do you have, Carver?"

"Sir, Miss Grant's cell has an incoming call."

The FBI had her cell phone? The last time she'd seen it was in her classroom on her desk. She'd assumed it had been confiscated as evidence since the terrorists had used it to converse with the police.

"The call is bouncing off one server after the other, sir. We believe it's *him*."

That bone-chilling cold she'd felt earlier crept its way through her body.

Krueger tucked a Bluetooth wireless earpiece into his ear. Then he took the cell phone and offered it to Claire. "Stay calm and listen carefully to whatever he tells you. We'll be monitoring the conversation, but we don't want him to know that."

The ringing abruptly stopped.

An anxious breath heaved past her lips.

Krueger thrust the phone closer to her. "He'll call back."

As if his mind were linked to the caller's, the ringing started again.

Claire took the phone. Her hand shook. She moistened her lips then flipped open the phone.

Her gaze collided with Krueger's as she placed it against her ear. "Hello."

"Claire Grant?"

She flinched. "Yes."

"You must go to Bellevue Square. Your task awaits you at the first-level children's play area. Do not deviate. Do not elicit help. No extraordinary measures like bulletproof vests or weapons. Nothing. I repeat, you must do as I say, unarmed and with no help. I am aware that you are not alone and that this call is being monitored. Do not allow your new friends to interfere. Keep this phone with you at all times. You have forty-five minutes, Miss Grant."

Krueger made one of those keep-going gestures with his hand and whispered, "Ask him what happens in forty-five minutes."

Claire couldn't think. The blood roaring in her ears from the frantic pounding of her heart made concentrating impossible.

"I don't understand your instructions. What is it I'm supposed to do at the mall?"

"You will receive additional instructions when you arrive at the play area."

She probably needed to ask other questions in order to keep him talking, but her mind simply wouldn't fix on anything.

"I'm…I'm not sure…"

"Hurry, Miss Grant," he interrupted, "or a child will die."

Chapter 7

"ETA is sixteen minutes, sir."

Claire rushed into the waiting elevator with Krueger and two other members of his team, Agents Talkington and Holman.

Her mind kept trying to make sense of what was happening, but somehow things wouldn't connect to form a logical pattern.

"I need the layout of the mall's first floor. We have only minutes to get backup into place." Krueger rattled off the orders as if nothing that had transpired in the past few minutes surprised him.

This was his job, she reminded herself. He probably did this kind of thing all the time.

But she didn't.

She looked at him, felt panic rising all too fast. "What's happening? I don't understand this."

Krueger shifted his attention to her, but before he could answer her question the elevator bumped to a stop on the lobby level.

He barked additional instructions to his men as he took her by the arm and herded her toward the hotel's front exit.

Seconds later they were en route to the Bellevue Square Mall. Claire watched in horrified amazement as the men made preparations. Special communication devices were positioned on shirt collars and tucked into ears. Krueger continued to dole out orders with a keenly honed focus that transcended the norm.

"Sir," Agent Talkington broke in, "the first-floor play area is a padded tugboat playground near Nordstrom's and Eddie Bauer."

"Let me know when we have backup in place. We need to take every possible precaution."

"What did he mean," Claire asked, her mind scrambling to catch up, "when he said I should hurry or a child will die?" All the possibilities, some far more horrifying than others, tumbled through her head.

Krueger met her gaze, his expression formidable and totally closed to assessment. She didn't want some prettied-up version of what was going down. She wanted the whole truth. Whatever was happening here she needed to understand.

"At this point, Miss Grant, we can only assume that he plans to lure you into some kind of trap using a child as bait."

Just when she'd thought she had reached her limit for feeling fearful or anxious, a new kind of terror detonated inside her.

"You're saying that a child is in danger right now. Because of me?"

This was her fault.

Her actions had set off this insanity.

All the pain and emotion from six years ago came barging in to combine with the mix of fear and worry she suffered here and now.

Hadn't she done the right thing back then? Hadn't she done the same yesterday at the school? Could she have acted any differently and ensured her sister's survival? Or Peter Reimes's survival from a cold-blooded terrorist?

"This isn't your fault, Miss Grant. This is about a terrorist. An animal capable of unimaginable atrocities. You saved the lives of your students. You didn't do anything wrong."

Confusion as to what to believe joined the already volatile mix of emotions. She wanted to believe Krueger was right. But if a child was harmed today because of what she did…

"He said I would die." She mentally reviewed the initial call she had received from Abdul Nusair. "Over and over again." She didn't actually get that last comment but she definitely understood the part about dying. "He doesn't have to bring anyone else into this." For the first time since this nightmare began she felt a sense of comprehension and determination. "If he wants me, he can have me." Her gaze locked with Krueger's.

"That's very noble of you, Miss Grant, but remember, we have no choice but to play by his rules. He set this game in motion."

She made up her mind then and there. If Nusair called again she would tell him as much. He didn't have to play this game with her. There was no need for anyone else to be put in danger. Whether Krueger agreed with her or not, she understood what she had to do.

A calm fell over her and she resigned herself to that fate. Her actions yesterday had been her decision. She would face the consequences.

"Miss Grant," Krueger said when she'd been quiet for a couple of minutes, "it's my job to see that you don't get hurt. Don't give up on me already."

Claire searched his face and those unusual green eyes. She sensed that he was feeling the weight of guilt now as well. Guilt for what he had proposed to her today. Guilt for what he knew he possessed no power to control. In that way he was just like her…they were in the same boat.

"Your job, Agent Krueger, is to stop Abdul Nusair. I know where I stand in this particular pecking order. I just want to make sure that no one else, especially a child, gets caught in the crossfire."

To her surprise he looked away. She wondered how it was that a man like Krueger, one who had no doubt seen the worst of the worst, could still feel remorse for collateral damage. To her surprise that idea made her admire him all the more.

Respect, she amended. She respected him. Admired was a little different. She had to remember that…for the next few minutes. After that it probably wouldn't matter one way or another.

The driver, Agent Holman, took the necessary turns that led into the mall's jam-packed parking lot. Agent Talkington directed him to the exit nearest their destination. Hundreds, maybe thousands, of people had been evacuated and moved well away from the entrance on this side of the mall. A wall of Seattle's finest as well as temporary barricades were in place for crowd control.

Claire's heart rate started to climb once more. She clutched her cell phone in her hand and prayed that Nusair would call back before anyone was hurt. She had to convince him to take her and forget all this staged drama. The circus wasn't necessary. This was between her and him; no one else needed to be involved.

His son was dead because she had gotten in the way of his plan. As much as she cherished human life, she felt no true regret for what she had done. If she had to repeat those moments a dozen times over, she would not have allowed Peter Reimes to die.

"Backup, including two snipers, is in place, sir," Talkington said. "The evacuation of the area is complete with the exception of five people trapped in the Eddie Bauer store."

Krueger and Talkington exchanged one of those looks that Claire knew meant she'd been left out of the loop on some aspect of the information.

"What about the child? Is there a child in danger at the play area? Is there any indication that Nusair is here?" She deserved to know what she was walking into here.

"We'll know more about the situation when we get inside."

He was hiding something from her. Claire may have only just met the man, but he had been far too direct with her on most things today for her not to notice the way he avoided eye contact now. She studied Agent Talkington. He knew whatever was going on. He'd carefully avoided looking directly at her as well.

As the driver parked the SUV, Claire steeled herself for what was to come. She had no idea what to brace for other than certain death.

Maybe that would be enough.

She got out of the vehicle, her gaze drawn to the looming mall entrance. Of all the times she had been here she had never considered this a place to fear other than for her credit card balance. Now she feared for her life…and for the possibility that an innocent child would be caught in the crossfire.

Krueger barked orders like a drill sergeant. Three more agents joined their group, gathering around her as if she were the president of the United States. She was completely cloaked by male bodies as they moved toward the mall entrance.

Once inside the routine continued. Claire couldn't see anything for the barrier of men all the way around her.

They stopped abruptly and the group of agents fanned out.

A base of operations had been set up. A wall about ten feet long and eight feet high shielded them from the playground and blocked her view. When she looked up she could see the second-level gallery. The place was deserted.

Claire tried to look around but too many agents

had crowded behind the makeshift wall for her to see anything on the first level beyond where she stood. Krueger and his team were looking at something she couldn't see.

She angled her way between two men and moved in next to Krueger. He was staring out a long, narrow window in the wall that wasn't a part of the mall's architecture. Something the backup personnel had put into place evidently.

Claire tiptoed up to get a better view.

The oxygen in her lungs evaporated.

A child, a little boy, no older than ten or eleven stood in the play area made to look like a tugboat. There was an odd bulkiness about the jacket he wore.

Where was his mother? Or father? Surely he hadn't been left there alone.

Alone.

Realization slammed full force into her chest.

Of course there was no one else in the play area. The mall had been evacuated.

Why weren't the police or the FBI moving in to help this child?

"Why is that little boy standing out there alone?" She turned to Krueger. "Why isn't someone helping him? Where are his parents?"

"Anyone who tries to get near him is stopped by a sniper."

Claire was confused. She remembered Talkington saying there were two snipers in place, but she thought they worked for the FBI.

Krueger wrapped those powerful fingers around her arm and squeezed, maybe to get her attention or maybe because he was afraid she intended to make a run for the boy. "There's someone shooting at whoever tries to help the boy. Our snipers can't get a position on the shooter. One mall security guard and one Seattle police officer have already been gravely injured trying to get to him. The police have the boy's mother in the Eddie Bauer store. Paramedics are treating her for injuries she sustained trying to get her son."

Claire started to shake. The tears welled in her eyes but didn't fall. The rising fury made her tremble so violently she had to wrap her arms around her middle to keep herself still. She had to do something. She looked around. All these trained agents and no one could do anything.

"This is crazy." She flinched at how loud her voice sounded in the quiet. "If enough of us make a run for the boy, surely the sniper can't get us all."

"Look again, Miss Grant," Krueger urged, his own pain evident in his expression now. "See the way the boy's shirt and jacket protrude in front. He has an explosive strapped to his chest. When the police officer was shot Seattle PD received a call from a man we believe to be Nusair. He warned that if anyone else went near the child, he would activate the charges. We have explosives experts standing by, but we can't do anything until we receive those additional instructions from Nusair."

Claire stared through the narrow window at the boy. "Oh, God." Now she understood this strange wall or shield. There was also a large container nearby. She'd thought it was one of the mall's numerous trash receptacles. Now, on closer look, she realized it wasn't—it was for bomb disposal. Some of the agents behind this shield with her wore SWAT gear with Explosives Unit emblazoned across their chests and backs. She hadn't noticed any of that until now.

How could they save that child?

Why would Nusair do this? He wanted his vengeance. But she was the one who had killed his son. Why didn't he strap explosives to her chest? Was he doing this because he knew that as a teacher she loved children?

"You'll need these."

Her attention jerked back to Krueger. He placed a communication device on her T-shirt, near the collar, then tucked what looked like a small hearing aid in her left ear.

"You'll be able to hear us and we'll be able to hear you."

"We have to do something," she pleaded. They couldn't just stand here. Nusair had said forty-five minutes or the child would die. Time was running out!

Her cell phone rang. The sound took her breath all over again. This would be Nusair, calling with additional instructions.

"Go ahead," Krueger said, "answer it. We're monitoring your calls."

Her fingers were cold and clumsy but somehow she managed to get the phone open. "Hello."

"Claire Grant, I see you have arrived on time."

"Why are you doing this?" She closed her eyes, hated herself for breaking down. Unable to stop the onslaught, sobs choked into her throat.

"Pay attention, Miss Grant, I will not repeat myself."

"I'm listening." She scrubbed at her eyes with the back of her free hand. "Tell me what to do. Just don't hurt the boy."

"The boy's fate is in your hands, Claire Grant. You must go to him. Stay on the line. I will instruct you further when you reach the boy."

"I'm going." She started to move, but Krueger stood in her path.

The standoff lasted only a few seconds.

In that fleeting moment she saw the defeat in his eyes.

He couldn't protect her.

He knew it and so did she.

Krueger stepped out of her path. The rest of the agents moved aside as well.

Claire cleared the shield and started toward the play area. The boy caught sight of her and started to sob even harder. She was certain he expected her to be shot as the others who'd come near him had.

Please, God, she prayed, don't let this child be hurt.

"It's okay," she said to the boy as she came closer.

Shock radiated through her as recognition kicked in.

Joey Denton.

He was in Darlene's class.

"Hi, Joey," she murmured. She tried hard to keep her voice from wobbling. "You doing okay?"

"Please help me, Miss Grant."

"Don't you worry, Joey, that's why I'm here. I'm going to get you out of this so you can be with your mom. Okay?"

He nodded. His eyes were red and swollen. She knew he was scared to death. Then she saw the tether. She'd wondered why the child didn't make a run for it. Now she knew. One end of the tether was attached to his right wrist with a plastic bracelet, thicker and far stronger than the kind used on hospital patients. No way could she get it off without a knife. It was too tight to slip over his hand.

"Now unzip his jacket," Nusair instructed.

She bracketed the cell phone between her shoulder and her ear and reached for the zipper.

"Be very careful, Claire, this could be a trap."

She jumped. Almost dropped the phone.

The voice was Krueger's. He'd spoken to her via the communication device tucked into her left ear.

She didn't respond. If she did Nusair would hear and she couldn't let him know there was any interference coming from Krueger's people. He'd warned her explicitly about that.

Slowly, her fingers trembling, she lowered the zipper on the jacket.

Her heart sank when she saw the bundled mass of gadgetry strapped to the boy's chest. Layers and layers of duct tape were wrapped around his thin torso, holding the device in place. A digital timer counted down from two minutes ten seconds.

"As you can see," Nusair said, "there are several wires in a variety of colors. All you have to do is select the right one to pull free of the mechanism and the timer will stop. Pick the wrong one and the device will detonate. If you run out of time, our game is over."

He severed the connection.

Claire's cell phone fell to the padded floor. She stared at the bundle. Did she dare touch any of it? If she had a knife she might be able to cut the whole bundle loose from his body and throw it....

"Talk to me, Claire. Let us guide you through this. Tell me what you see."

Krueger.

"It's a *bomb!*" She had to stay calm and think. "It's…a jumble of different items. A nine-volt battery…what might be a transistor of some sort. Lots of electrical tape and wire nuts and…oh, God, the timer is ticking down really fast."

The timer blinked menacingly at her, one minute, forty-eight seconds.

There would never be enough time.

"Claire! Listen to me. Don't touch anything yet. Our bomb squad tech Bob Jackson is going to take you through this."

"What color are the wires, Miss Grant?"

A new voice…

She moistened her lips, drew in a much-needed breath and forced herself to focus.

"All different colors. Red, black, white, green, yellow." Her foot started to tap. She was running out of time.

Joey's breathing was ragged, his chest rising and falling with monumental effort. Claire locked gazes with the boy. Please, God, don't let him breathe too deeply. This thing could go off.

"Okay, Miss Grant, listen very carefully to me."

Claire stilled, held her breath.

"Look all the way around the device. You see the battery, the transistor and there should be a small solar fuse in the mix. It'll be a small square or rectangular device. There may be an electrical lightning-bolt symbol on it for ID purposes."

"Yes, I see it." She squatted down to get a better look at the bundle.

"Do you see anything else?"

"Duct tape. Something beneath all the gadgets. It's like a block of…I don't, molding clay maybe. I'm afraid to touch it."

Several seconds of silence followed.

"What do I do now?" Didn't they realize her time was running out? "There's only sixty seconds left. Somebody tell me what to do!" She was screaming.

One look at Joey's face and she wanted to tear out her tongue for letting him hear her panic. She held her breath. Told herself to calm.

"Miss Grant," Bob said, his voice somber, "this is an IEP, an improvised explosive device. It will not detonate if it is disconnected from the power source, the battery. Do you understand me? It *will not* detonate when separated from its power source."

She tried to see what he meant, but she had to be sure. "I'm not sure what you're telling me to do." He had to give this to her in more straightforward terms. "Power source? Do you mean the battery or…or what?"

"Pull the wires loose. Without the connection to the battery the timer will stop. The battery is the power source."

She reached for the wires.

Her hand froze.

"Wait! He said if I chose the wrong wire—"

"Miss Grant, I can't see what you're seeing, but from what you've described to me this is a home-made device using C-4, a simple timer, a battery and a solar fuse. The C-4 will not detonate without an igniting charge. No power source, no detonation. I think he's bluffing. Pull the wires loose. Do it *now.*"

Claire stared at the jumble of colored wires. "But what if you're wrong?"

"I'm going out there."

Krueger.

"Sir, you can't go out there!" Talkington's voice blasted in her ear.

Claire whipped her head around just in time to see Krueger make a lunge for a massive potted plant about six feet from the shield.

Bullets pinged against the marble floor next to the potted plant.

"Tell him to go back! Tell him to go back!"

Claire's gaze collided with the boy's as he shouted those words over and over. He was trembling. His eyes were huge.

Twenty-nine seconds.

"Miss Grant." The technician's voice sounded in her earpiece. "You're running out of time. Yank the wires loose from the battery. If you don't do it now, the initial charge will detonate and then the C-4 will blow. You'll die. The child will die."

...the child will die.

Claire stared at the timer.

Ten seconds. Nine.

She grabbed a handful of the wires and pulled as hard as she could.

Nothing happened.

Five seconds.

Her fingers twisted in the final two wires.

She stared into the boy's tear-filled eyes, prayed she wasn't making a mistake and ripped the final wires loose.

Chapter 8

Two seconds.

The timer stopped.

Unable to speak, Claire sat back on her haunches, hugged her arms around her knees and didn't move.

She couldn't move…she couldn't tell what had happened…

There was no explosion.

Only the silence of complete shock.

"Am I going to die?"

The boy's frightened voice broke the tension.

Claire managed a shaky smile. "I think we're okay now, Joey."

Everything happened at once after that.

Krueger and his team were suddenly on top of them. No more flying bullets from the sniper. Bob, the technician, and one of his associates removed the bundle from Joey's torso, placed it in a containment canister and hurried away.

Claire watched as Joey was reunited with his mother. He was really okay.

It was over.

"Miss Grant, are you all right?"

She looked up into Agent Krueger's now-familiar green eyes. He'd run out into the open, risked his life to help her and the boy. He'd been as good as his word. She wanted to answer his question, but somehow she couldn't form even the simplest syllable.

Her knees buckled. Krueger caught her just in time.

"Medic!"

A woman wearing a paramedic's uniform came rushing up to Claire with a medical bag in hand.

Krueger and the paramedic guided her toward the nearest bench. "Let's get you off your feet, Miss Grant."

"I'm fine. Really."

"Why don't we make sure about that?"

Claire sat through the routine screening. Her heart rate had slowed and she could breathe comfortably now but she still felt disconnected, as if her mind and body were separate entities.

Krueger divided his attention between her and the ongoing investigation.

When the paramedic finished her examination, she patted Claire on the arm. "You're going to be fine, Miss Grant."

The paramedic walked over to Krueger and spoke quietly to him. Claire didn't hear what she said, but she presumed that the woman passed along the same information she had given her. She would be fine. No permanent damage.

Not physically anyway.

She might not sleep for about a hundred years without having extreme nightmares.

Krueger came over and sat down on the bench next to her. "Miss Grant, we're going to transport you to a safe house now. We took out Nusair's sniper before he could escape, but if Nusair was here he slipped past our net. We believe any threat in the area has passed, but I don't want to risk your continued exposure in this setting."

He stood and offered his hand. She placed hers in his and allowed him to help her to her feet. She didn't like having to rely on anyone else but she felt pretty darn shaky just now.

The team working directly for Krueger gathered around her once more as they exited the mall.

Two SUVs waited right where the sidewalk met the asphalt. Krueger opened the rear driver's-side door of the first one and Claire climbed in. He took the front passenger's seat. Talkington drove and Betty Nance slid in next to Claire. The crowd of shoppers watched from behind their barricades. She wondered how long they would be forced to wait before they were able to get into their vehicles and leave. It wasn't likely that anyone here would forget this shopping experience.

"Are we going back to the hotel now?" It was the first coherent sentence she had managed to get out in the last several minutes. Krueger had told her where they were going but for the life of her she couldn't remember what he'd said.

"No." Krueger didn't bother turning back to look at her. "That location may be compromised now. Anytime we make a major move motivated by the enemy, we'll change our location just in case. We have a safe house prepared for your arrival."

Claire leaned back and told herself to relax. But she couldn't. "What if I hadn't survived and Nusair was still at large?"

"We do the best we can to make contingencies for every scenario, Miss Grant."

During those tense moments in the mall he'd called her Claire. She wondered now if he'd done that to get her full attention. Now he wouldn't even look at her and it made her uneasy. Was he hiding something or was he fighting his own reaction to what had just happened?

The muscle flexing in the hard line of his jaw gave her an answer. No matter how many times he'd done this it wasn't easy for him either. Claire didn't know why, but somehow that comforted her just a little.

Dusk had fallen over the city. The lights twinkled dramatically. She lost herself in the beautiful skyline with its soaring Space Needle and Mount Rainier as a majestic backdrop.

She'd come here all those years ago to escape the pain and the memories. Her life in Seattle to this point had been quiet and pleasant. She'd made lots of new friends. This city was home now. From day one she'd made it a point to get to know her new home. The first couple of years she'd spent every weekend that she didn't work on her house exploring the neighborhoods.

For all that time she had felt completely safe. Safe and happy.

Until now.

The driver made lots of turns and did a significant amount of backtracking. She had no idea where they were headed, but she definitely recognized when they cruised the same block twice.

Their destination eventually became clear when she spotted the headquarters of Amazon.com high atop Beacon Hill overlooking downtown Seattle and Puget Sound.

She'd considered buying in the Beacon Hill area before she fell in love with the little bungalow in her funky, eclectic neighborhood in Fremont.

Would she ever be able to go back there?

Why was she still alive?

A frown tugged at her brow.

Nusair had had a sniper in the mall. Why hadn't he shot her when she managed to disable the bomb? Or even before?

Would the fact that a bomb-squad technician had talked her through disarming the bomb make Nusair even angrier? He'd warned her about getting help from her new friends. Yet he'd done nothing about it when he had the opportunity back there.

If he wanted her dead…wanted his vengeance, why hadn't he taken it? Not that she was in any hurry for that to happen.

Claire Grant, you will die for your transgression. Over and over again.

She turned her hands palms-up and stared at them. Had there been something on the device…anthrax or something that might kill her later?

Was that why she felt so exhausted now?

Her fingers tightened into fists and she closed her eyes to shut out the thoughts. She wasn't thinking rationally. She didn't know why she was still alive. Or why the sniper hadn't taken a shot at her. The only thing that mattered was that Joey Denton was safe.

More questions came to mind when she thought of Joey. Why Joey? Was his selection happenstance? Out of all the kids in Seattle, did he just happen to be in the mall at the wrong time?

That seemed like an awfully big coincidence to her.

The SUV slowed and made a turn dragging Claire's attention back to the present. The day had completely given way to night while she'd been distracted by her disturbing thoughts.

How could less than thirty hours have passed since all hell had broken loose?

For the first time since she had walked out of that school alive yesterday she considered that her sister would likely be aware of what had happened by this point. For nearly six years Claire had lived in Seattle without anyone from her hometown knowing where she'd moved to. Now the whole world knew.

She didn't know how she felt about that. Somehow the anonymity had been reassuring. Here, with only herself to answer to in regards to the past, she'd felt able to move on without looking back.

For six years she had rarely thought of that night.

Now everyone from her past who watched the news knew that she was responsible for a second man's death. Nothing like showing off how well you've done for yourself.

Krueger opened the door and waited for her to get out of the SUV.

Claire slid out of the seat. As her feet settled on the pavement, she took in the area. She didn't recognize the neighborhood, but it was dark. Maybe she would notice something familiar in the daylight. The house was two-story colonial-style brick with nice big columns. Pretty swanky place.

A white picket fence, a little fancier than the one she had at home, wrapped around the yard. She couldn't tell much about the landscaping. There were only about four other houses on the short cul-de-sac. The driver had parked the SUV in the colonial's driveway.

As they approached the house the garage door hummed to life and began to rise. Once they were inside the garage, Talkington pressed a button and sent the garage door back into the closed position.

Krueger led the way through a door that opened into a large kitchen. Two more agents, both dressed in the official FBI uniform of navy or charcoal suits with coordinating ties, waited inside.

In the kitchen Krueger turned to Claire. "Agent Nance will see you to your room. You should take a break. We'll talk later."

"Thank you."

Krueger touched her arm. When she'd met his gaze, he said, "Keep in mind that no one died today. That makes what happened a success rather than a failure."

She nodded and he let her go. She understood that he wanted to make her feel better about the situation, but that was something she simply couldn't do right now.

Nance led her down a long hall that ended in an entry foyer. From there she took the stairs to the second floor. When they had reached the second door on the right in the upstairs hall, Nance stopped.

"This will be your quarters until this is over." She opened the door and went inside the room.

Claire followed. The room was nice. Smartly decorated in subtle shades of blue and gold.

"There's an en suite bath." Nance indicated one of the doors on her side of the room. The other was probably a closet. "The items you wanted from your home have already been unpacked for you."

"Thank you, Agent Nance."

Nance smiled—it was the first time Claire had seen any of the agents do that—and left the room.

Not that she didn't believe what the agent had

told her, but Claire needed to see for herself. She went to the closet. Sure enough there were the clothes she'd asked for. In the bathroom all her toiletries were lined up on the counter. Back in the bedroom she checked a couple of dresser drawers and found her underwear and pajamas.

Along with her nightshirt and box of chocolates she found something she hadn't expected. Her one and only family photo album. She kept photo albums at school of activities she and her students had done together, but, at home, she had just one. This one. She smoothed a hand over the aging cover. It was the one possession of sentimental value that she owned. Pictures of her and her family, of her parents years ago before they'd passed away and of her sister.

The album was her one connection to the past besides the diary. She couldn't bear to lose it. She tucked it away in the drawer with her nightshirt. She couldn't look at it now…too painful. Knowing it was there was enough.

For long minutes she stood in the middle of the room and tried to decide what to do next.

A shower? Or just crawl into the bed.

She had no appetite. Unbelievably.

Hey, if she survived this and lost weight, she could go on *Oprah* and announce a new kind of diet, the Run-from-the-Terrorist diet.

Ha-ha.

A knock on the door made her jump.

Claire pressed her hand to her chest and hauled in a calming breath. There was nothing even remotely funny about her situation. Then again, if she didn't make jokes she might very well cry.

She didn't want to cry.

She walked over to the door and opened it. No point asking who it would be, the person on the other side of the door would be Agent somebody.

Krueger.

She blinked. A little surprised to see him so quickly. He'd said they would talk later.

"Agent Holman has gone out for pizza. According to your file you like cheese pizza."

Her file?

"This file contains information on what I like to eat?"

Amusement flashed in his eyes then morphed into an outright smile. "Vanilla-bean ice cream. Chocolate mousse. Cheese pizza. Burgers, well-done, mustard and pickles only."

Her cheeks heated with mounting mortification. "Oh."

"May I?" He gestured to the room.

She stepped back from the door. "Sure."

When he stepped inside, the bedroom felt way smaller. He looked around. "Is this room to your liking?"

"It's fine."

Those intense green eyes settled on her. "You have everything you need?"

"Yes."

"Excellent."

Claire moistened her lips. Her mouth felt dry all of a sudden. "Were any of Nusair's people spotted as we left the mall?"

Krueger pushed the lapels of his jacket aside and settled his hands at his waist. He'd loosened his tie again. He looked tired, but even tired he couldn't be called anything but handsome. Funny that she would notice anything so insignificant as that right now. Maybe she just needed something else to occupy her mind. She'd read about cases where extreme stress brought on escapism fantasies. God knew, reality was getting more and more unbearable. But then, she'd been fixating on details about him since she'd first laid eyes on him.

"I'm afraid not. Nusair's people are very good, Miss Grant, and, unfortunately, they have the element of surprise on their side. They act, leaving us with no choice but to react. Not the best scenario for us."

She nodded. She could understand that.

"If you're feeling up to it," he went on, "I'd like to bring you up to speed on what we're doing. So you'll be assured that we're on top of the situation."

The situation. The most-wanted terrorist in the world wanted her dead. She wasn't sure much of anything he said would be reassuring, but she supposed that as long as she was alive there was always hope that tomorrow would be better.

"First, we've identified the hiding place the sniper used at the mall. That isn't much but knowledge is power and we now know a little more about how Nusair is planning to carry out his vengeance."

As much as she wanted to be impressed by the Bureau's work, she hoped they knew more than a little. To say so would be unkind as well as ungrateful. Krueger and his men were trying to help her. Still, that he kept his face wiped so clean of expression made her wonder if there were things he didn't want her to know.

"We're running scenarios on how Nusair chose his victim. Since the boy wasn't one of your students, we're narrowing down whether or not the boy is the child of a friend or someone you know from church or some other social activity. Or if he was picked just because he was your friend Darlene Vernon's student."

Claire was shaking her head to all of the above but she abruptly stopped. "Is Darlene okay?"

"Yes. We beefed up security at her home. She's fine."

Thank God. "What about…" Claire chewed her bottom lip a second, considered whether calling directly would be the right thing to do. Would her sister even take the call? Maybe not. But she had to be sure her family was safe. Whether her sister wanted anything to do with Claire or not, she couldn't let this situation become her problem, too. "What about my sister and my niece?"

"Both are fine."

Relief spread through her extremities, taking with it some of the strength provided by the adrenaline fear had prompted. The people she cared about were safe. That was all that mattered at the moment.

"We're now looking at the possibility that Nusair selected the boy because he was an only son."

That got Claire's attention. "Like Habib?"

Krueger nodded. "We think that might be the defining factor. We're already running down a list of all the boys enrolled at your school who are only sons."

"Can you protect them all?" This whole thing just kept getting bigger and bigger.

"We have everything under control, Miss Grant."

For the first time since she'd met the man, Claire allowed herself to search his face and those unusual eyes openly. The covert thing just wasn't working. She needed to see some sort of reaction, some indication of how he felt other than the facts he relayed. And there were questions she wanted to ask that suddenly seemed important to her. She felt extremely lucky to have such a competent agent on her case. But she had a feeling that luck had nothing to do with it.

His tension visibly escalated at her blatant scrutiny.

"How did you come to be on this case?"

That muscle she'd seen flexing in his jaw before reacted. His hands drifted down from his waist to hang at his sides. "That's somewhat of a long story, Miss Grant. I'm sure you wouldn't find it interesting at all."

Now, there was a hint of something. He let his fatigue show in his voice.

She hunched her shoulders then let them fall. "I don't have anything else to do while I wait for the pizza to arrive." She felt sure he did, but perhaps he would indulge her need to know.

That same weariness she'd heard in his voice made an appearance in his eyes. "I've been tracking Abdul Nusair for years." The admission wasn't spoken with any pride, more with a long-harbored frustration. "I've been this close—" he held his thumb and forefinger about an inch apart "—but he always gets away. He treats our close encounters like a game designed for his entertainment."

A memory pinged Claire. "He said that today." How could she have forgotten? "Something like, if you run out of time our game will be over."

Krueger closed his eyes and shook his head. "He's a cold-blooded killer, Miss Grant. When the right opportunity presents itself, he loves nothing more than dangling a person's life on the end of a string just to make him or *her* sweat."

She didn't have to ask. Claire knew instinctively from Krueger's words and voice that Nusair had yanked his chain more than once.

"Is that why he let me live today?" She hadn't been able to get that idea out of her head from the moment that timer stopped counting down the seconds.

"I'm certain of it. He enjoys the fear you experience. He wants more."

Another realization became crystal clear. "That's why he said I would die over and over again." Her gaze connected with Krueger's. "He's going to do it again."

"That's a strong possibility. He insisted that you keep the cell phone with you at all times. He'll likely call again. Probably sooner rather than later. The only question is how he'll go about his next move."

"Maybe next time you'll be able to catch him,"

she suggested, the conversation they'd had earlier about her being an *asset* zooming into dramatic focus. Her first assessment had been right. She was the bait. As much as she hadn't meant to sound bitter, the words had come across that way. She could see it in his eyes.

"Maybe," he told her, effectively evading the question. He hitched a thumb toward the door. "We have your cell phone charging downstairs."

She hadn't even thought of that. In fact, she would have walked away from that play area in the mall and left it lying on the floor if someone else hadn't thought to pick it up. She hadn't exactly been in her right mind at the time.

A light tap on the open door drew Claire and Krueger's attention across the room.

Talkington looked a little hesitant to enter. "Just thought I'd let you know that the pizza is here."

"Thank you," Krueger said, his tone dismissive. When Talkington had moved away from the door Krueger turned back to Claire. "Just so we're clear on this, Miss Grant." His gaze leveled on hers, the cool, calculated intensity back. "If there were any way within my power to make this go away for you, I would personally see to it that it happened. Make no mistake, I want Nusair badly, but I don't want him if it means sacrificing your life. Unfortunately, we don't have the luxury of making that choice. He has made the choice for us both."

Claire knew he was right. "I believe you, Agent Krueger. After today, I know you will do whatever you can to help me get through this. And if, during the stressful moments that are likely planned for me, I come off as ungrateful, please know that's not the case."

"Then I believe we're in agreement, Miss Grant."

They were.

She relaxed considerably. "Why don't you call me Claire, Agent Krueger? A man who knows my favorite ice cream should certainly call me by my first name."

A smile toyed with one corner of his mouth as he yielded just a little. "Does that mean you'll call me Luke?" The same amusement that tugged at his lips, made an appearance in his eyes. "I can't recall the last time anyone called me by my first name."

The moment was such a departure from seconds before, but it was also contagious. Claire felt her own lips form a smile. "I thought Agent *was* your first name."

"Very good, Miss…Claire."

As he turned to the door, she placed her hand on his arm. He stared at it a moment before meeting her eyes. "Just so you know," she said, needing to make sure he understood her position, "if the worst does happen I won't hold it against you. I did what I did to protect my students because it was the right thing to do. I don't regret my decision and I'm prepared to face the consequences." This was a place she'd come to know long ago. Regret was a completely useless and destructive emotion.

Admiration flashed in the depths of those green eyes. "I'm quite certain I've never met anyone quite like you, Claire." His hand came up. She held her breath as he tucked an errant wisp of hair behind her ear. His fingers grazed her cheek, made her shyer. "You puzzle me."

He stared deep into her eyes a moment longer, then dropped his hand back to his side. "We should join the others before the pizza disappears." As they moved toward the door he added, his tone back to that neutral place he appeared to prefer, "I've worked these operations before. Agents on all-nighters will eat anything that doesn't eat them first."

Claire, with Krueger right behind her, made her way back to the staircase and then down to the first floor. Her nerves still jangled from his touch. She kept telling herself how foolish her reaction was, but it didn't do a lick of good. She noticed there were at least two agents in every room she passed, all with pizza and soft drinks.

The smell of garlic and cheese had permeated the air, making her stomach rumble in less than ladylike fashion by the time they reached the kitchen.

No one had touched the cheese pizza. Several others, ranging from meat lovers' to supreme, slices missing, sat around the large kitchen table.

Claire grabbed a slice while Krueger reached into the refrigerator. He handed her a diet cola. She imagined that her preferred soft drink was in her file as well. As much as she hated dieting, she would rather consume her caloric intake in chocolate than in sugar-packed colas.

A ringing cell phone snapped her attention toward the bar that separated the kitchen from the large family room.

"We have a call coming in on Miss Grant's cell," Agent Holman announced.

Claire stared at the phone the agent held in his hand.

What if it was Nusair again?

Her heart rammed into her throat.

"Have we ID'd the caller?" Krueger demanded.

"Can't pin it down, sir," Agent Betty Nance explained. "Someone's rerouted Miss Grant's calls through a server that blocks all our attempts at caller identification or the originating location of the call."

Agent Talkington rushed into the kitchen with a wireless, hands-free earpiece for Krueger.

Krueger tucked the earpiece into place and turned to Claire. "Take the call, Claire." His voice was gentle, much more so than when that first call had come in.

Claire placed her pizza and cola on the table, the chill of fear already making her fingers numb and shaky. She'd barely blinked and Holman was suddenly standing next to her offering the phone.

Praying it wouldn't be *him,* Claire accepted the phone. Her fingers trembling, she opened the flip top and pressed it to her ear. "Hello."

Chapter 9

"Claire?"

Darlene.

The sense of relief at hearing her friend's voice proved so acute that Claire pressed her hand over her mouth and squeezed her eyes shut to hold in the overwhelming emotion.

Struggling to regain some semblance of composure, she scrubbed the dampness from her cheeks and managed a shaky, "Hey."

"Where are you? Are you okay? My God…the news…the whole thing at the mall was on the news! I've just come from the Dentons'. I can't believe this happened to Joey. His father is such a nice man. It's just awful. What kind of animal would do this?" When she paused and Claire remained silent, Darlene asked, "Claire, what's going on?"

Claire looked to Krueger. He'd heard Darlene's end of the conversation the same as she had. She wasn't sure what she could tell her friend.

"Tell her," Krueger murmured, "that you're safe and you'll contact her as soon as the threat has passed."

If the threat passed.

The unexpected understanding in his eyes gave her the strength she needed.

She mentally buttressed herself for telling her friend something other than the whole truth. "I'm okay." She allowed her gaze to rest on Krueger. Mentally held on to him for support. "I'm in a safe place. Don't worry, I'll call you as soon as this is…over."

"You're sure you're okay?"

Darlene wasn't ready to give up. She must have heard the uncertainty in Claire's voice. They knew each other far too well.

"I'm fine. Don't worry about me. Just take care of our kids."

"Please be careful, Claire."

"I will."

It took every smidgeon of strength Claire possessed to hold back the emotions pounding inside her as she said goodbye to her friend…knowing it might be the last time. She closed the phone. Holman was there instantly, taking it from her hand. Keeping it charged and handy was essential since that was the only connection to Nusair. Claire felt numb…something she seemed to be experiencing a lot lately.

"You should eat," Krueger encouraged. "Before the pizza gets too cold."

She shook her head. "I'm not hungry."

Claire left the kitchen, hurried up the stairs and closed herself up in her assigned room. She didn't want to talk to anyone right now. She just needed to be alone. And, oddly, for the first time in her life, she had no appetite whatsoever. If she weren't on the verge of tears she might actually laugh.

More than anything right now she needed to feel free of today's events. She needed to escape somehow. But she couldn't. There was no place to go that Nusair wouldn't find her. She had promised to try and help trap him, but how were they ever going to accomplish that when all they could do was react?

No more thinking.

She went into the bathroom, undressed and huddled in the shower until the water ran cold, then she went through the blow-drying and straightening routine with her hair. At this point she didn't actually care how her hair looked, but the familiarity of the chore was somehow comforting.

Once she'd pulled on her nightshirt, she opened that box of special chocolates she'd kept for an emergency and popped a delicious piece into her mouth. The gratification was instant and soothing. Deciding one would never be enough, she took a couple more and crawled into bed. She promised herself that things would be better tomorrow.

Now she was lying to herself.

Things wouldn't be better tomorrow.

She had killed a man.

No matter how tightly she shut her eyes she could still see him lying there on her classroom floor.

She replayed every moment of the events that led up to that frantic instant when she'd knocked the weapon away from little Peter Reimes and toward Habib Nusair.

No matter how she played out the scene, there simply had been no way to save Peter without doing what she had done.

But Habib, still a kid himself, had been a human beneath that veneer of hatred that compelled him to commit such heinous acts of terrorism. She had killed another human being, however cruel and lacking in compassion.

A part of her would never forgive herself.

His own youth had made him reckless. If he'd had one of his minions holding the boy while he forced her to shoot, she wouldn't have been the one to kill him. He might have even been the one to escape with his life. But he'd been full of vile arrogance and determined to be the one to hold the target. Probably wanted to watch her face as she was forced to do the unspeakable.

Where was his mother? Why hadn't she or someone taught the man the true meaning of compassion? The value of human life? Was anyone actually mourning his death? Well, other than his father with his evil plan for revenge and, as far as Claire was concerned, that didn't count.

How had Habib come to be the ruthless killer she had observed in her classroom? Was he merely following in his dad's footsteps?

Maybe she was wrong to blame the rest of his family for the way Habib had turned out. She didn't know his family, other than Abdul, and she only knew him by reputation.

Claire had known her brother-in-law's family.

The Farmers were good people. No matter that their son abused his wife, they still loved him. In their eyes, Claire had murdered their son.

Just as she had murdered Habib in Abdul Nusair's eyes.

How long would it take the guilt to fade?

She still felt remnants of sadness when she thought of Tad Farmer, even after six long years of trying to put it behind her. But the sadness wasn't the same thing as regret or guilt. She felt guilty for taking a human life, felt sad for those who would mourn the loss. But she couldn't possibly regret her actions.

How could she have made any other choice?

Tad Farmer had entered her home, with a weapon, intent on harming her sister.

Habib Nusair and his followers had entered her school intent on harming her students. Habib himself had ordered Principal Allen's murder. A pang of grief stabbed deep into her chest. Habib would have killed more students before SWAT got inside had she not stopped him.

And that had only been the beginning.

She had done the right thing.

She would definitely do it again if the circumstances called for such action.

If Nusair didn't kill her first.

"Claire."

Her eyes didn't want to open.

"Claire, we have to go."

A hand shook her shoulder. This time her eyes flew open. The light from the lamp on her bedside table cast a dim glow over the man who shook her again, a little harder this time.

"Get dressed. We have to leave. Now."

The urgency in Krueger's voice had her throwing the covers back.

"What's happened?"

He sat on the bed next to her. He placed a steadying hand on her shoulder. "We've picked up on some chatter between some of Nusair's suspected followers that he's planning a strike on a safe house in Seattle before 7:00 a.m. We aren't inclined to believe that he has our location but we're not going to take the risk. So we're leaving as soon as you can be ready. Don't worry about packing. Your things will catch up to you later."

She wondered if it was that simple. As calm and soothing as his voice sounded, he looked worried. More worried than she had seen him. "How could he find us?"

"He couldn't," he said flatly, with no hesitancy. "Not unless he's using some technology we don't have yet to capture a signal from your cell despite our measures against his doing just that. This may just be a bluff to try and force us to react. But we're not going to take the risk."

His gaze dropped to her mouth then.

He licked his thumb, then swiped at something on her chin. Heat glimmered inside her, momentarily chasing away the cold reality she'd awakened to.

One corner of his mouth quirked. "I see you found the chocolate."

She glanced back at her pillow, saw the melted chocolate on the pillow case. She'd fallen asleep before finishing that last piece. The heat she'd felt all over at his touch suddenly zeroed in on her cheeks.

"I did." She met his eyes, felt warm all over again at the way he looked at her. "Thank you."

He cleared the interest she was certain she saw from his eyes. "We should get moving." He stood, backed up a step.

She climbed out of the bed, abruptly aware of how high up her thighs the hem of the nightshirt fell. "Okay." When he didn't move, she ducked past him and rushed around the room, gathering jeans and a sweatshirt and her sneakers. Socks? Where were her socks? She checked under the covers and found them. Then she backed toward the bathroom door. "I just have to change and I'll be ready."

As if he'd suddenly realized he should leave, he gestured to the hallway. "I'll wait outside for you."

Claire retreated to the bathroom and dragged on her clothes. She ran a brush through her hair. There wasn't time to evaluate what had happened with Krueger. He was right. They had to hurry. She finished up, grabbed her purse and met Krueger in the hall outside her room. She followed him down to the first floor.

Everyone was already gone.

At her questioning look, Krueger explained, "An advance party moved about fifteen minutes ago. The others are waiting outside."

"Where are we going?" she asked as he escorted her out of the house and to the SUV standing by in the driveway.

"To another location in the city. We can't move too far out of Seattle."

"In case Nusair has another round planned for today," she guessed.

Krueger opened the rear passenger's door and she climbed in. He slid into the front seat and nodded for the driver, Talkington, to go.

When he still failed to address her concern, she reworded her question, "You think that's going to happen, don't you?" She scooted to the other side of the backseat so she could see his profile.

The beat of silence that followed her question was fraught with mounting tension.

This couldn't be good. Fear brushed the base of her spine.

"We know he is."

"How?" She reminded herself to breathe and willed her voice not to shake. "How do you know this? Has he called?"

A long agonizing moment passed before he answered. Every second of silence registered in the hard lines and shadowed angles of his face. This wasn't as easy for him as he'd like her to believe.

"A boy was taken from his home."

Claire's fear morphed into horror.

"Who?"

"Chad Wade."

A student in Sherry Everett's class. Another fifth-grader from Whitesburg Middle.

"When did this happen?" The question came out in a calm voice, though she didn't see how she could speak so rationally considering the hurricane of questions and concerns whirling in her head.

"About two hours ago."

The digital readout on the SUV's dash indicated it was 4:00 a.m. Despite police protection, the boy had been taken from his own home, maybe his own bed, in the middle of the night.

Another student from her school.

An only son. He didn't have to say; she knew.

"Has there been any contact from Nusair?" She didn't know why she asked that question, a second time at that. If he had called Krueger would have wanted her to answer the call.

"No, he hasn't called yet."

But he would call. When he was ready. When he'd choreographed the perfect moment of terror for her to endure, then he would call.

"You're sure it was Nusair?" Some part of her

wanted to hang on to the possibility that this might not be about Nusair or what she'd done.

But deep down, she knew.

"It was Nusair."

Anger flared inside her at his continued evasiveness. "How can you be so sure?"

"Because he left his calling card."

"What calling card?" She hadn't heard anything about this. Why was he keeping her in the dark? Making her dig for every answer?

"He marked the front door of the Wade residence with an X using blood from the father."

A new jolt of tension shook her. "Is Mr. Wade dead?" The horror just kept mounting. How could any man be so ruthless?

"He's still in surgery but the prognosis is good."

Claire closed her eyes and banished the brutal images of the child being snatched from his home and the father being injured. She couldn't dwell on those things or the fear would consume her. They had to find a way to stop Nusair. But how? He stayed far away from the dirty business he orchestrated. At least till now he had. How could they take him down if they couldn't find him? If he didn't get close enough?

Wait. Something about this calling card evidence wasn't right. Didn't add up. "If this is the first time you've seen this, why would you call it Nusair's calling card?"

"He marked the Denton home similarly."

His father is such a nice man. What kind of animal would do this?

Now she understood what Darlene meant when she'd said that earlier. "Joey's father was attacked, too? Why didn't someone tell me about this?"

"There was no need to upset you any more than you already were."

Her anger spiked, making her want to scream or tear something apart, maybe a little of both. "Next time, Agent Krueger, you let me decide what I need to hear and what I don't."

Krueger didn't respond to her warning. She didn't care whether he said anything as long as he did what she asked. She was as much a part of his investigation as anyone. She had a right to know.

Claire stared out the window into the darkness. She ignored the sparkling city lights and the street signs. She didn't care where they were taking her. It didn't matter.

Chad Wade was missing. Most likely taken by a heartless terrorist.

And she was the reason why.

Later—she didn't know how much later since she'd been lost in her thoughts—she became aware that the vehicle had slowed considerably, then it turned into a driveway. Another house. The agents on Krueger's team were already there. She recognized the sleek black SUVs that were carbon copies of the one in which she rode.

She didn't wait for Krueger when the vehicle stopped. She got out and walked toward the door. What was the point in protecting her when they couldn't protect the innocent kids from her school?

The more she thought about the situation the angrier she became.

Yes, she'd killed Nusair's son. But he was a terrorist. A killer who had murdered her principal and was about to murder one or more of her students. She was glad he was dead. The world was a better place without him.

If that made her a bad person, then so be it.

No one got in her path as she stormed up the porch steps and to the front door. She didn't even knock, she just went on inside.

She stopped and stared defiantly at Agent Nance. "Where's my room?"

Looking startled, the agent glanced at some point beyond Claire's shoulder—to Krueger probably. Then she said hesitantly, "Upstairs, first door on the right."

Claire marched up the stairs and went straight to her room.

It faced the back of the property, which was likely the point. There was only one window and, just as last time, there was an adjoining bathroom.

Home sweet home.

She plopped down on the bed and considered her options.

She laughed, a wholly pathetic sound. What options?

She didn't have a single choice in this ongoing nightmare.

Except one.

A rap on her door proved perfect timing.

She didn't have to ask who it was, she knew. So she walked over and opened the door.

Krueger. Big surprise.

"We should talk about this."

"You're right." She opened the door wider. "We should talk."

Crossing her arms over her chest, she moved to the center of the room and waited for him to close the door. Once he settled his attention on her she dropped the bomb, so to speak.

"I want you to find a way to get in touch with Nusair and tell him you'll trade me for the boy." She lifted her chin defiantly when his expression hardened for battle. "I want this to end today. We should have done this already the way I wanted to."

"Don't you understand that it won't ever end as long as Nusair is alive?"

Yes, she understood that perfectly but she had no control over the bigger picture.

"This isn't about political correctness or military strategy. This is about a ten-year-old boy whose life I'm not willing to risk. It's me that Nusair wants. I killed his son. He wants his revenge. It's as simple as that. If we give him what he wants, Chad Wade and the rest of the students at Whitesburg Middle will be safe."

Krueger moved a step closer to her. She saw the smallest of cracks in his cool, calm veneer. "For how long? A day? A week? Maybe a month or a year? Abdul Nusair has terrorist cells in more than a dozen major cities in the U.S. We need to know how to stop whatever he has planned. We can't do that by throwing away the first connection we've had to him."

She took a step toward him, determined to make him sweat. "So it's okay if Chad Wade dies as long as we save the masses, is that what you're saying?"

He flinched. As she'd hoped, Krueger was rattled.

God, how could she toss that at him? How did a mere human measure the loss of one life against the loss of thousands? It simply wasn't meant to be that way. She was not emotionally equipped to make that kind of decision. Yet, here she was taking a stand in a situation the full scope of which she could not possibly hope to understand. She was wrong to oversimplify the difficult task facing this man.

Special Agent in Charge Luke Krueger looked weary. Whether his fatigue was physical or mental, she couldn't say. At that moment she felt the full weight of his station. As horrifying as her position was just now, it didn't come close to comparing to what he must feel. This had to be his worst nightmare.

"That may be the way it feels," he agreed, his voice low and placating. "I know. But that's not the way it is. Every cop this city can spare and two dozen Bureau agents are working to find that child. Nothing we do is going to stop Nusair from carrying out his sick scheme. Even if we turned you over to him, the chances of the boy being freed unharmed are zero to none. Nusair's MO doesn't allow for it. He doesn't leave loose ends or witnesses." The pain she saw in his eyes leeched into his voice. "He kills everything in his path. What you saw him do in that mall was about torturing you. That's the only reason you and that child are still alive."

The more passion infused his words, the closer he came to her until she had to look up in order to maintain eye contact.

"I will do everything in my power to see that the boy is rescued. I promise you that."

She found herself watching his lips. It was crazy. And yet somehow she needed to feel something besides this stifling fear and overwhelming outrage. She needed to feel anything but that. He stood so close, those green eyes were so intent on her, that she couldn't help feeling the urgency of his words…the passion in his determination to stop this animal and somehow to protect her and the children. She needed to touch that…to strengthen herself with his determination.

"I will do all I can. You have my word."

Standing here, desperately needing someone to hold her and make her forget the fear and the outrage, she realized for the first time in her life that she was completely alone. She had no family that claimed her. Sure she had Darlene and her friends at school, but she had no one else. No one who loved her the way a woman should be loved. No one to hold her the way a woman wanted to be held.

No one.

Wouldn't that be a terrible way to die?

Alone and unloved.

"I need you to hold me, Krueger." She hadn't meant to say what she felt out loud. But she needed this too badly to pretend she hadn't meant the words.

He didn't hesitate. Those strong arms went around her and pulled her close against his chest. Claire laid her cheek there and closed her eyes.

He smelled good. Vaguely of the starch the drycleaners had used on his shirt and more deeply of a citrus fragrance. His chest felt solid and steady beneath her, something she had needed for a long time. Powerful arms shielded her and she desperately wanted to revel in that awesome strength. The rhythm of his heartbeat soothed her, made all the bad feelings dissipate.

"I'm sorry this happened to you," he murmured. "I wish I could make it go away."

The longer he held her, the more relaxed and secure she felt. But it was his words that touched her the deepest. The moment wasn't overtly sexual, but she couldn't deny an ache of longing. She'd missed this kind of connection with another human. It was a shame that it had taken such tragedy to bring her to this wondrous place again. The warm, heady feel of a strong male body. The distant, yet urgent pull of desire.

It didn't matter that she scarcely knew Krueger. The events of the past fourteen or so hours had forged a bond that, hard as she tried to ignore it, had been there almost from the first moment they'd met.

A keen awareness simmering beneath the skin. Why couldn't they have met under other circumstances? He was one man she could honestly say would be a challenge to dissect on an intellectual level.

She liked that he was complicated and intriguing.

Was that the need to de-stress speaking? She didn't usually have an eye for police officers or men in other high-risk occupations when it came to prospective boyfriends. If she faced facts, she would confess that she hadn't had a boyfriend in ages. Period. She busied herself with the children. With advancing her work skills and supporting the community in various ways such as Habitat for Humanity.

This moment was pure indulgence, pure selfishness.

And she wanted it to go on and on.

She wasn't the only one feeling the heat. The tension in his muscles had become palpable. His body grew more rigid the longer he held her. When his hands started to move slowly over her back, she knew for certain she wasn't in this alone.

But he would never make the first move. He wouldn't go beyond the line that his professional credentials had drawn.

She lifted her face to his, let him see the desperation in her eyes. His lips were so close. She could feel the urgent pull of his need with the same electrical intensity as she did her own. That tug was every bit as clear in his eyes. He wanted this as much as she did.

He kissed her, just a soft brushing of his lips over hers. She wanted more. Tiptoed to make the contact complete.

The world and all its troubles spun away when he took charge of the kiss. Her hands, flattened on his chest, moved up and around his neck. She wanted to feel her breasts pressed against his chest, her pelvis melded to his. She made it happen.

Still, it wasn't enough.

Not nearly enough.

She wanted—needed—so much more.

Several staccato raps on the door sent Claire stumbling back from his arms.

It gave her some amount of satisfaction that Krueger looked as dazed as she felt.

He took a moment to compose himself, reached out and gently stroked her cheek with the pad of his thumb, then turned to the door.

Claire didn't move. Heat still shimmered through her body; her lips still burned from his kiss. She smoothed a hand over her hair and tried to catch her breath. This wasn't exactly the time to be distracted.

Just something else she had no intention of regretting.

Holman rushed into the room as Krueger opened the door.

"Sir, Miss Grant has a text message from Nusair."

Krueger took the cell phone from the agent's hand. He studied the small screen, then showed it to Claire.

There is a surprise waiting for you at your modest bungalow.

"Is it possible that Chad Wade is there?" Claire's heart started to thunder in her chest. Why the text message? Where were her instructions? Did Nusair assume she would go to her house when she got this message? Was that the reaction he wanted?

Krueger shoved her phone into his jacket pocket and took her arm, his touch gentle yet firm. "Let's go."

The drive to her Fremont residence took more than a half hour. The whole way Claire kept trying to block the vision of Chad on her porch with a bomb strapped to his chest. She didn't want him to be hurt. But if he was there, and most likely he was, he would play some part in Nusair's sinister game.

She kept glancing up at Krueger. Several times she caught him looking back at her. He was worried. He did a very good job of hiding his emotions, but she could see the concern in his eyes.

Had that one kiss made him as vulnerable as it had her?

Over and over she told herself that it was just a kiss. A physical release of tension that two people had needed. Nothing more.

Except it had felt like more.

Maybe she had imagined those sparks she'd noticed when they first met. She'd fixated on physical details instantly. There had been a little something between them even then. Or maybe it was just she who had felt that shift in chemistry. After all, it had been a really long time since she'd even been attracted to anyone. Keeping to herself ensured a great many things, not the least of which was staying away from heartache.

She was thirty, almost thirty-one. Could she go on with the rest of her life, assuming she survived, avoiding that kind of relationship?

Didn't she deserve to have someone?

Or was staying single and unloved her self-imposed punishment for killing her sister's husband?

Now there was a truly twisted possibility.

Claire shook her head at her own self-analysis.

She was a textbook case of neurosis.

The SUV pulled up to the curb in front of Claire's house.

Thank God poor little Chad wasn't tethered to her porch rail. She'd imagined the worst-case scenario all the way over here.

She reached to open the door and an explosion rent the air. The vehicle shook and shuddered. Debris flew toward her window as she stared in shock at the unexpected eruption.

"Get down!"

A powerful hand came against the back of her head and shoved her into the floorboard as debris rained down on the SUV like baseball-sized hail. Glass shattered and pelted her back.

When the bombardment stopped, the pressure from the hand lifted allowing her to move once more.

Claire rose up slowly, settled onto the edge of the seat and turned to stare out the shattered window.

Smoke rose from what remained of her house. Nothing but a few rocks and planks.

Several seconds passed before she comprehended what had just taken place.

Her house had blown up.

Nusair had bombed her house.

Terror clutched at her heart.

Where was the boy?

Chapter 10

"I want her out of here!"

Claire shook her head, tried to understand exactly what he was saying. Her hearing was a little off. Krueger was right there. His voice sounded low despite the facial expressions that indicated he was shouting.

The explosion.

She stared at her house.

That was the reason she couldn't hear very well. The explosion had dulled her hearing the way a camera flash will temporarily blind.

There was absolutely nothing wrong with her

vision, however. Her house was now a pile of smoldering rubble. The kind seen in a war zone.

"The boy." Fear snarled like an angry beast inside her. "We have to see if Chad was in there! If Nusair brought him here…"

Please, please don't let him be in there.

Krueger was out of the SUV.

"Take her back—"

"No." Claire wrenched her door open and slid out. She staggered on wobbly legs. "I'm not going anywhere. This is—was—my home."

"Nusair's people could still be close by," Krueger warned, one hand on her arm, ready to marshal her back into the SUV. The fear in his eyes was palpable…startling.

She twisted free of his hold. "I don't care. I need to know if that child was here. Stop fighting me on this, Krueger."

He took a breath. She saw his chest expand and deflate with the harsh force. He surveyed the block, first left, then right. Dawn had sent pink and purple streaks across the sky, highlighting the senseless devastation on the ground.

Lights had come on in the neighboring homes. People were beginning to creep out onto porches to get a look at the trouble. Thankfully the other houses didn't appear damaged. Smoldering debris had flown all over, landing here and there in nearby yards.

No matter what he said, she wasn't leaving.

"Stay right behind me," Krueger ordered, his expression reflecting the sheer desperation she felt. "Do exactly as I say."

She nodded.

Sirens in the distance signaled that the fire department and maybe ambulances, definitely the police, were on their way.

How could this be happening in her neighborhood...to her home?

Claire glanced back at the SUV with its shattered windows on the passenger's side that faced her house. She swallowed at the lump of fear lodged in her throat. They were damned lucky they hadn't been injured.

Or killed.

Flaming pieces of what had been the interior of her home were tossed around her yard and against the picket fence she'd painted just last month. Broken glass and chunks of furniture had landed in the oddest places, like in the bird fountain and in flowerpots holding her tender pansies.

Krueger kept her close to him, not daring to let go of that connection...his hand clutching hers or his arm around her shoulder. His constant watch and vigil to protect her made her want to turn

into the protection he offered and just let go of the
worry…of the pain.

He wouldn't allow her to get close to what was
left of the house, which wasn't much. The fire
trucks arrived and worked quickly to drown the
few lingering flames.

She heard someone say that it would be hours
before they knew for certain if anyone had been
in the house. Hours. Again she said a quick prayer
for Chad and his family. Surely Nusair would have
wanted to taunt her more than this. Let her see the
child trapped or something like that…the way he
did at the mall.

Then again, the *not* knowing was almost worse.

Out of the blue she remembered her last face-
to-face conversation with Darlene.

Take care of my place for me.

Another wallop of fear crashed in on her.

"I need your phone!" She turned to face
Krueger, her fingers fisting in his shirtfront. "Your
phone. I need your phone!"

If Darlene wasn't home…oh, God. What was
her cell number? Claire knew it…she had to think!

Krueger seemed to shelter her with those broad
shoulders and powerful arms as he passed his cell
phone to her. Claire let him, didn't want to feel
this vulnerable, as she stabbed in Darlene's home

number. She had to start over… more slowly this time.

Claire listened to the ringing on Darlene's line.

If she were home she should be up and getting ready for school by now. No wait, there wasn't school today, was there?

Another ring.

More of that fear tightened around her chest.

Please let her be okay.

"Hello."

Relief flooded Claire, making her sway. "Darlene, you're home?"

"I was just getting out of the shower. Is everything okay?"

Claire stared at her house. No, nothing was ever going to be okay again. But she couldn't break down about that. She had to keep it together. "Well, my house just blew up, but other than that, I'm good." Save for a terrorist for a stalker, she didn't add. But that was no big deal, right?

"Are you okay? Jesus, Claire, this is horrible. You mean it just blew up? Just now?"

"Yes." She wanted to say no she wasn't all right. But her friend didn't need to hear that. "I'm fine. I just…" What a mess. What would she do, assuming she survived this crazy ordeal?

"I have to go, Darlene." She wanted to move closer to where a crew wearing fireproof gear and using special tools was now sifting through the rubble that used to be her house.

"Be careful, Claire," her friend urged.

"I'll try." Claire closed the phone and gave it back to Krueger. Television news vans had arrived and reporters were already shouting questions.

The unmistakable sound of her cell phone rose above the growing commotion around her.

Claire's gaze collided with Krueger's.

She'd just spoken to Darlene.

This wouldn't be Darlene.

Talkington rushed over. "It's him." He looked from Krueger to Claire and back. "We've identified the number he's calling from. We just can't locate it."

Whoever was monitoring the calls on her phone had passed the information along via the communications link the agents appeared to wear twenty-four hours per day. If Talkington said it was him…he had confirmation. It would be Nusair.

Rising terror nipped at Claire as she realized this call would be about Chad.

Krueger passed her cell phone to her.

Claire took a breath and opened it. "Hello."

"Too bad about your nice little house, Miss Grant."

Outrage abruptly elbowed aside the fear. "Where's Chad?" That was all she wanted from this lowlife scumbag. She refused to *chat* with him.

"You look so upset, Miss Grant. Is the FBI treating you poorly?"

She stopped…turned all the way around, her gaze scanning the faces in the crowd…the windows of the neighboring houses.

He was here. Watching her. Reveling in the result of his evil deeds.

With nothing more than a few gestures Krueger ordered his men to form a boundary in both directions along the street. He grabbed Claire by the arm and started hauling her toward the closest SUV.

"You shouldn't be in such a hurry to go, Miss Grant. Don't you want to see if there is anything left to salvage? Or have you lost everything?"

Claire froze at the SUV's open door. Nusair had just admitted something significant to her. He'd lost everything. His son had been *everything* to him. He wanted her to feel the same loss.

She wondered what he would say if she told him that she had already lost everything…. She'd lost it all six years ago. But if he didn't already know about her sister, she wasn't about to give him any more ammunition. Let him dig for whatever he found out about her.

"It's me you want, Nusair," she said, her voice steady and calm for a woman who'd just watched her home go kaboom. "Let the boy go. I'll come to you. Name the place. I'm ready right now."

She wrenched free of Krueger and backed away from the SUV, stood out in the open where Nusair could easily see her.

Krueger reached for her again but she avoided his touch, held up her free hand to back him off. She had to do this.

"Come on, Nusair. Why go through all this risky foreplay? You don't need these games. Tell me where you are and I'll come to you. Right now. I'm what you really want. I'm all yours."

"Get in the vehicle, Claire," Krueger ordered as he grabbed her arm again.

She yanked free of his grip, arrowed him a warning look.

"Your protector doesn't agree," Nusair countered. "And I'm afraid your offer, tempting as it may be, is much too easy for all concerned. Recent developments have given me a second agenda. I've waited a long time to get your new friend in this very position. A position that requires a most difficult choice. Perhaps this will be the moment and I will enjoy double the pleasure."

Her gaze connected with Krueger's.

"What does that mean, Nusair?" She was tired of his riddles.

"You must go to Port Townsend, Claire Grant.

Look for the ferry named *Olympas*. Wait on the boardwalk for my instructions. You must hurry. You have only forty-five minutes."

Her dread escalated, overtaking all other emotion.

"Hurry, Claire Grant, or the child will die."

He severed the connection.

Claire propelled herself into the SUV Krueger had been attempting to prod her into. The windows were still intact in this one and Talkington was already behind the wheel. "Did you get that?" she demanded of Krueger who was climbing into the front passenger's seat.

He didn't have to answer her directly. He was busy issuing orders via his communications link and those orders were answer enough. Then he turned to Talkington. "You're going to have to lose any of the media that attempts to tail us."

"Will do."

Claire twisted around in her seat and watched as they drove away. Sure enough, two reporters fell in behind them. The news channel logo on one of the vans she recognized, the other she didn't.

"We only have forty-five minutes," Claire reminded. Port Townsend was at least twenty minutes away. And finding the right dock would take time. They didn't have any time to waste.

No one responded to her reminder. They knew as well as she did what was at stake.

She wrung her hands together and prayed this situation wouldn't be even worse than the last one. She had to calm down. If she didn't get a grip, she wouldn't be able to do what had to be done. Chad Wade was counting on her. She had to do this right for him.

Closing her eyes, she tried to picture the ferry. She was familiar with the area. But for the life of her she couldn't remember any relevant details. Where exactly was the *Olympas?*

She was wasting her energy worrying. Krueger and his men would have all the pertinent details well before they arrived. She knew that about his team. They were extremely efficient. By the time they'd reached the mall last time, Krueger's people had every single relevant detail. The only thing she needed to do now was brace herself for what was to come.

Nusair's comment about how long he had wanted to get Krueger in a position to have to make a difficult choice nagged at her. What had he meant by that? Surely Krueger had some idea since he'd heard Nusair's end of the conversation the same as she had. There really hadn't been time for him to explain what Nusair meant…or maybe he didn't intend to discuss with her his private issues related to this terrorist.

She tried to push the topic out of her thoughts, but it wasn't going anywhere.

When they had given the reporters the slip and were within ten minutes of their destination, Claire decided she should ask Krueger about it. If there was relevant history between Krueger and Nusair, she had a right to know.

"What did Nusair mean when he said he'd waited a long time to get you in this position?"

For several seconds she felt certain he wasn't going to respond, then he started talking. "Nusair is only attempting to distract you, Claire. You shouldn't put any stock in his offhanded comments."

He wouldn't look at her when he said this and his response had Talkington cutting a sidelong glance in his direction. This only confirmed Claire's suspicion.

Krueger had just lied to her. Maybe only by omission, but in her book it was a lie just the same.

She couldn't help but feel disappointment. He'd kissed her, for heaven's sake. She'd thought they had connected. Surely she hadn't been that wrong about what she'd felt. Still, he'd just lied to her.

Maybe she'd been wrong about what the kiss meant. About what she'd seen in his eyes. About him.

The port came into view, and again, everyone in the vicinity had been moved far away from the

water where the ferries were docked. A line of
Seattle's finest, as well as a temporary barricade,
was in place. It amazed her even now, considering the circumstances that had brought her here,
how quickly the authorities could work in a situation like this.

Tension vibrated inside her, reminding her that
the gorgeous Olympic and Cascade Mountains in
the distance might very well be the last things
she ever saw. At least she couldn't complain about
the setting. If a girl had to die, this was as close to
heaven as could be found on this earth.

Her gaze swept over the broad, deep Puget
Sound and the tiny islands and ragged peninsulas
beyond. She'd fallen in love with this place the
first time she saw it.

How could anything bad happen at such a beautiful place?

When the SUV stopped she started to get out.

"Wait," Krueger ordered.

He was listening, she realized. Someone on his
team was likely giving him an update via their
communications link.

"We can't go beyond the boardwalk," he told
Talkington, his voice resigned. "Same scenario as
the mall. Nusair has a sniper keeping anyone from
going past that point. *Dammit.*"

Claire surveyed the boardwalk and the pier beyond. He had to be using one or more of the boats. Maybe the *Olympas,* her destination. She took a long slow look around. Then again, a sniper as good as Nusair's could be anywhere within a couple hundred yards.

Half a dozen agents appeared at her door and Krueger gave her the go-ahead to emerge from the vehicle. Once she was rigged for communications she was ready to go.

"We need a moment," he said to his people.

The other agents backed off, leaving him shielding her in the V-shaped space made by the open vehicle door.

He looked pretty much anywhere but at her. "If I let you do this—"

"Wait." She held up a hand to stop him right here. "We don't have a choice. You know that."

His eyes locked with hers then. "He's going to kill you, Claire. You know that."

And then she knew just how much his stoic determination had cost him. He wanted Nusair; that was absolutely true. But he didn't want Claire to pay the price. His need to protect her went deeper than the professional…she could see that…could feel it radiating from him.

"We're wasting time," she reminded him, some part of her deeply grateful that he'd showed her just how much he cared. She'd known his compassion equaled his passion, but this confirmed his feelings about the job and about *her.*

"Sir?" Talkington stepped toward them. "We're ready."

Krueger held her gaze a moment longer before he moved aside and let her go.

Claire moved forward, again surrounded by a protective shield of agents, until she reached the point where the sniper fire prevented anyone else from going forward with her. She cleared her mind of all other thoughts. Nothing else could get in the way right now.

The first step onto the boardwalk had fear clamping down around her chest, making a deep breath impossible.

When a bullet didn't tear through her, she moved forward a few more feet toward the ferry, then waited as Nusair had ordered.

She didn't make any unexpected moves. Didn't do anything that might even remotely be construed as aggressive.

The sound of seagulls drew her attention to the sky where they seemed to float in midair, drifting high above the water.

The sky was amazingly blue…perfect.

A nice day for staying alive.

She'd made it to the gangplank to the ferry when Krueger's voice murmured in her ear.

"Five years ago he killed one of my agents." The anguish in his voice squeezed at her heart.

Claire moistened her lips and managed to haul in a decent breath. "I'm sorry."

"I had to make a choice," Krueger said. "Let my agent die or let Nusair walk."

The realization of what he'd done stole the breath Claire had managed to draw in.

"The standoff lasted several minutes. Nusair was convinced he'd won, that I wouldn't risk a fellow agent's life. He laughed. Asked me if I would really let him shoot her. When I hesitated about lowering my bead on him, he shot her. My agent died and he escaped anyway. It was my fault. The decision was mine."

Claire wasn't sure what to say to that. *Sorry* wasn't nearly enough. She was sure Krueger never closed his eyes without reliving that moment. She thought of her own situation six years ago. Maybe they had something far more than physical attraction in common after all. Too bad it had to be the kind of damaging event one didn't want to talk about, much less share.

"I won't make the wrong choice this time, Claire."

She told herself not to read too much into the words. Too late. He'd already had an effect on her. She doubted that the feeling would fade so easily, assuming she was still breathing when this was over.

Her cell phone rang.

"Hello."

"You have less than ten minutes, Claire Grant. If you hurry, perhaps you'll save the day yet again."

Nusair ended the connection.

Claire shoved the phone into her jeans pocket and rushed toward the ferry.

She looked around the boat as she boarded. Then she saw him. The boy was bound to a support beam in the main seating area where the tourists lounged for their trips around Puget Sound.

Immediately she could sense that this time was totally different.

"Tell us what you see, Claire."

She produced a shaky smile for the boy as she approached him. "You remember me, Chad? Miss Grant from school?"

He managed a jerky nod.

"You don't need to be afraid now. Everything's going to be okay."

But it wasn't.

Worry gnawed at her as she surveyed the situation.

It was no homemade explosive rig this time.

She crouched down in front of the boy and looked over and around the sophisticated device. "It's a sleek black box. About four by nine inches. Maybe two inches thick. The timer is built into the box. There's just over seven minutes remaining."

Lots more time than at the mall, but she had a bad feeling that it wouldn't be nearly enough.

"Help me," Chad whimpered. "I want my mom and dad."

Claire squeezed his arm reassuringly. "We'll get them on the way over here. Don't you worry now. I'm going to fix this."

Please, God, get me through this one more time.

Whatever it took, she would convince Nusair to take her and leave the children out of this.

She couldn't bear to see another child go through this horror.

Then again, if she didn't stop this timer, she wouldn't be in a position to negotiate.

"Can you open the box?"

It was Bob Jackson. The explosives technician.

Claire placed her hands on the cool surface of the box, slid her fingers all the way around the edge. She attempted to pry it open at what looked like a seam where two pieces were sandwiched together.

It wouldn't budge.

"I don't think so."

She tried to look behind it, but it was strapped around the boy's torso with a wide strap that apparently latched inside the box itself. Whoever had made this, designed it for the purpose of ensuring it couldn't be removed from its wearer.

But the box had to open. Somehow.

"Chad."

His swollen, tear-filled eyes met hers.

"Did you watch them put this thing on you?"

He shook his head. "There was a bag over my head."

She managed another, somewhat shakier smile. "Don't worry, Chad. We'll figure this out."

Four minutes, fifty seconds.

"I don't think I can get this off," she admitted, hoping the boy wouldn't pick up on the panic edging into her voice. "Even if I had scissors, I don't think they'd cut through this strap."

"Look around the ferry, Claire."

Krueger's voice.

"There should be something you could use as a makeshift lever to pry the box open. Nusair said you couldn't bring anything with you. He didn't say you couldn't use what was already there."

He was right. She moved around the large open area. Checked each table and behind the counter. Opening the drawers there, she found a flashlight and a screwdriver.

"I have a screwdriver," she said for Krueger's and Bob's benefit. With her find in hand, she hurried back to Chad and knelt down in front of him. "It won't matter how I pry on this thing, right?" It wasn't like there were that many places to try. Just that one continuous seam all the way around the edge of the box.

"You don't have a choice, Miss Grant," Bob said, his voice grave.

That wasn't a yes, but he was right. She set the tip of the screwdriver at the seam and met Chad's gaze. "Just hang on."

He nodded, his eyes round with fear.

Claire pried as hard as she could. The screwdriver slipped twice, poking Chad. He cried. She cried. But she didn't give up.

Again and again, she struggled with the damned box.

It wouldn't budge.

Frustrated, she shook her head, dropped her hands to her knees. "I can't get it open."

One minute twenty seconds.

They were going to die.

Somehow this time her heart rate remained steady; her pulse didn't run away. Surrender. Nusair had defeated her. She and this poor little boy were going to die.

"Try to get it off him, Claire," Kruger urged. "Strip his clothes off. Slide the whole thing, strap and all, down his body."

Hope bloomed. That could work.

"I'm going to try to get this thing off, Chad. So don't get worried when I take your shoes and pants off, okay?"

He nodded.

She tugged off his shoes, then unzipped his jeans and shoved them down.

The device was strapped around him and the support beam. She tugged at the strap, tried to slide it down his torso.

The box moved.

Thank God.

Chad started to help her then.

She tugged, he pushed.

They had to hurry.

Forty-one seconds.

Chad shuddered and cried out in pain.

"What's wrong?" She kept tugging. Had to get this damned box off him.

"It hurts!" he wailed.

Then she saw the blood.

Running down his bare sides.

She scrambled from one side to the other to see where the blood was coming from.

The inside of the strap had ripped through his skin…. Tiny razor-sharp spikes protruded from the underside of the damned thing.

Those bastards!

The cuts in his skin weren't deep, just enough to be painful and bring the blood.

But getting the strap down the rest of the way was going to be a problem.

She moved back in front of him. "Chad, I know it hurts. But we have to get this off."

Twenty-three seconds.

He nodded his head that he understood. Her fingers shook as she took hold of the strap again. She pulled. Chad wailed.

Her breath came in ragged spurts. She couldn't stop or they would run out of time. She tried to put her fingers between the strap and his skin but there wasn't enough room. She couldn't get her fingers in there. There was no other choice.

Her heart pounded.

He screamed out in pain as she shoved the strap down his hips.

The timer kept ticking down.

Chad hit at her.

She fell back on her butt.

"It's okay," she assured him.

He swung at her again. He'd held out as long as he could. Now he was completely hysterical.

"Wait, Chad! Let me help you."

"Claire, what's happening? How much time do you have left?"

Nine seconds.

They weren't going to make it.

She gripped the strap, pulled harder. Chad pounded at her. His fist connected with her temple, but she didn't stop.

The box fell to the floor.

She grabbed the boy in her arms.

He kicked his feet free of the contraption.

Two seconds.

She lunged upward, the boy clinging to her.

Zeroes blazed across the timer.

Too late.

Chapter 11

Claire's heart stopped in her chest.

Time seemed to stand still.

Nothing happened.

No explosion.

Chad sobbed against her shoulder.

The warm feel of blood was plastered between her arms and his slim torso.

"Claire! Talk to me! What's going on in there?"

Krueger.

"I'm coming in!"

She pivoted, held the boy firmly and ran.

The idea that the sniper was likely still on

location didn't stop her from running as fast as she could. Then her gaze locked on Krueger barreling up the boardwalk.

"Go back!" she screamed.

A bullet pinged on the wooden walkway near Krueger. He dodged but didn't slow.

God, he was going to get himself killed. But the gunfire had suddenly stopped.

He ran straight to her, drew her into the shelter of his big body and ran like hell.

Someone took the child from her.

Agents were all around her before she could blink.

Sirens wailed in the background.

"We got the sniper," Talkington said. "That last blast of gunfire gave away his location."

"Is he alive?" Krueger demanded, his arm still keeping Claire close.

Talkington shook his head.

The sniper was dead.

But Chad was alive. *She* was alive.

Claire stared back at the ferry.

It was still there. Didn't blow up like her house had.

Two agents decked out in full SWAT gear and members of the bomb squad rushed onto the ferry.

Why was she still alive?

Why did Nusair keep playing this insane game?

She heard someone say, "The boy's mother is en route to the scene."

Thank God the child was safe.

"You okay?"

She faced Krueger. The worry in his expression should have calmed the rage she felt rising, but it didn't. Nor did the idea that he'd risked his life to come to her aid. There was only one way to stop this.

"No. I'm not okay. I want this over. Today. I don't want any more children to go through what this boy just suffered."

She didn't wait for his answer. Waving aside the paramedic who attempted to approach her, she strode over to the SUV she'd arrived in. There was no need for her to hang around here. Nusair wouldn't be here. He would be far away watching the fun from some place safe.

To hell with that.

She didn't even wince at the curse word. She was sick of his games.

No more being the victim.

She glared at Krueger as he approached. No matter what he thought, no matter how badly he wanted to nail Nusair, he would do this her way.

"No more safe houses. I want to go back to the hotel where all those files are and I want to formulate a strategy for getting this bastard."

Krueger looked surprised at her choice of words. She didn't care.

He sighed, then motioned for Talkington and Holman. "Let's go."

They loaded into the SUV and drove away from Port Townsend and Puget Sound.

Claire didn't look back.

Nusair wasn't coming out of hiding for these little petty games orchestrated to scare a mere schoolteacher.

No way.

He was too smart.

Their only chance of nailing him was if she refused to play anymore and forced Nusair to take her on personally. A suicide mission. It was the only way.

She knew it and Krueger knew it.

All she had to do at this point was make him admit that she had the only feasible solution to this nightmare.

Then they could mastermind their own plan.

On the fourteenth floor of the plaza, Claire took a few minutes to clean up. She couldn't bear the blood any longer.

Chad Wade was fine. As far as they could tell he, like Joey Denton, had not sustained any serious abuse beyond the surface wounds from the bomb rigging.

She had just learned that the sleek black box strapped to Chad's chest hadn't even contained an explosive. The whole set-up had been designed to torture her…to scare her half to death.

Well, it had worked.

Darlene had called. Everyone at school, including the students, were praying for her. The boys who were the only male children in a family had all been pinpointed and were now in protective custody. Claire felt confident that the boys were thrilled to have days off from school. Their families were likely far less thrilled and way more terrified.

But they needn't worry. This was going to end today.

One way or another.

Claire exited the luxurious bathroom and moved through the conference room where she'd first been briefed by Krueger. What had once been the second bedroom of the suite, on the other side of the parlor, had been transformed into a sort of situation room.

Everyone waited for her there.

"I have questions."

The team seated around the table shifted their attention to her as she entered the room and took a seat at the end of the table opposite Krueger.

His gaze remained fixed on her as she settled

in. She was glad she'd chosen the navy sweater with a conservative neckline and the comfortable jeans. She needed all the comfort she could manage on her side. Judging from Krueger's eyes, this was going to be an uphill battle all the way.

He had no intention of yielding control.

He said nothing, waited for her to begin.

"I understand that Nusair wants vengeance for his son's murder. And I'm the one who killed him. So I'm clear on why this is happening. My first question is why would Nusair devote so much of his attention to someone as irrelevant in the overall scheme of things as me? Doesn't he have real terrorist work to do? What about all those cells you told me about?" This final question she addressed directly to Krueger.

Fixing her with his green eyes, Krueger answered her. "Allowing Kaibar to blow his cover and be captured was Habib's fault. Remember, that's what set this chain of events in motion. Habib was in charge of the cell here so any misstep would have been a reflection on his leadership ability. That kind of mistake would be a major humiliation, especially considering he was Nusair's son. His youth and ambition only made things worse when he decided to attempt to right the situation by negotiating for Kaibar's freedom."

Getting himself killed, Claire finished for him. That was what had started this whole thing.

"We've gathered intelligence in the past twenty-four hours," Krueger went on, "that indicates there is some unrest among Nusair's followers. Apparently some of his top people are worried and impatient for the same reason you just stated. As you suggested, they're concerned about how much time Nusair is focusing on you and the loss of his son."

That was good in her opinion. The problem was, Krueger didn't appear happy about it. His ability to keep her from reading him was apparently malfunctioning. Either that or she had simply learned to see past the front he kept in place.

"Considering that," she offered, "I would think that Nusair would want to wrap this up pretty quickly now."

Claire looked from Krueger to the others, one agent at a time, to gauge their reaction to her theory. The folks around the table were far too good at maintaining poker faces for her to hope for some inkling of their thoughts on the matter.

"That's my thinking," Krueger confessed, startling her with his agreeable tone. But the glimmer of worry in his eyes belied his words. "We're already building reaction scenarios for what may come next."

This was the part that annoyed her. "I don't want to react. I want to *act*. Chad Wade was taken from his own home just a few hours ago. If I don't do something now, Nusair will have another child to use as bait before dark. I can't let that happen."

Krueger leaned forward, braced his arms on the table and settled that intense, troubled gaze on hers. "We don't want that to happen either, Claire. But this is Nusair's playbook we're dealing with. He makes the rules. If we don't follow those rules he might very well blow up a whole school."

She hadn't thought of that. But then she wasn't trained for this kind of thing. Krueger knew what he was doing; she didn't have a clue.

She surveyed the somber faces around the table. These people fought the bad guys for a living. She was just a schoolteacher. What did she know about stopping a terrorist? How had she hoped to make this happen? Who was she kidding?

"There has to be something we can do," she urged. "Waiting for him to make a move can't be the best thing."

Defeat started to drag down the determination she'd worked up after this morning's horror. She couldn't just sit here like this and let another child be thrust into the worst kind of danger by this madman.

"There is one possibility that might work," Krueger offered.

Anticipation shored her crumbling resolve even if he didn't look overly thrilled. "So you do have a plan?" Why hadn't he told her this already? Maybe because she hadn't given him a chance to talk.

"We had hoped that Nusair would be so beside himself with grief that he would screw up and get too close in an effort to have his revenge, but that hasn't happened."

"But now you have a plan," she prompted, hoping he'd get to the point soon. The suspense was killing her.

"Yes. We need a couple of more hours to work out the details, but we have a plan."

The sense of relief she felt was very nearly overwhelming. But did they have a couple of more hours? It was anybody's guess.

"Can you tell me about this plan?" If it involved her, she wanted to hear the details.

"Let's wait until we have the profile worked up, then we'll initiate the operation phase, including full strategy briefings."

"When do you expect to have everything worked out?" She didn't like being left in the dark. Time was wasting. Why couldn't they move forward right away? That he avoided looking directly at her now as he spoke had her uneasy.

"Within the next two hours."

Krueger stood; his team did the same. He thanked those assembled and walked out.

Confusion won out over the worry and anticipation. What had that been about?

Claire pushed back her chair and got up. Somehow he'd managed to agree with her completely and, yet, to tell her nothing at all. She was still just as in the dark as she had been before. Why was he suddenly backing off? She went to find Krueger.

He was standing in the parlor, staring out the massive window overlooking Seattle. The drapes had been left open today. He didn't bother turning around when she came into the room.

"Why are you working from here instead of the local Bureau office?" She knew they had one in Seattle. She'd meant to ask the question before, but other things, like staying alive, kept getting in the way. This whole setup seemed a little odd compared to what she'd seen in the movies and on television crime dramas. He'd mentioned something about security but she had a feeling there was more to it than that.

He took his time turning around. Those green eyes that had stolen far too much of her attention the first time she'd looked into them rested heavily on hers now. "We maintain close contact with the local office. Our experience, however, has been that working from a separate location gives us a certain level of focus and operational security we can't get any other way. We talked about that."

Krueger didn't trust anyone and certainly didn't want anyone getting in his way. He could say what he liked, but she understood that about him if she understood nothing else. But underneath all that hard professional veneer, he was worried. Worried about not getting Nusair this time. Worried about her.

"No leaks this way," she proposed. "You have your own hand-selected, personal team. Everything is under your control, no variances, no deviations. When did you stop trusting the rest of the world?" It was funny how she'd recognized this to some degree about him all along, but it only now connected for her on a conscious level. Something else they had in common.

"Five years ago."

When Nusair killed his agent.

"Mistakes were made. Information leaked. We were blindsided and someone died because of it."

She moved a few steps closer to him. "This someone, was she important to you?"

"All my agents are important to me." Krueger's guard went up. He was on the highest level of alert.

"But she was special to you when the workday ended." This must be part of the reason he wanted to nail Nusair so very badly.

He searched Claire's eyes as she drew closer and then he surprised her by telling her the truth. "There was a time when she was more, but we had ended that relationship. She had plans of moving into a senior position and our relationship stood in the way."

"But you still worked together." That seemed strange. Why not move on completely? Claire had never been in that position but she felt sure it would make life a lot easier to make a clean break.

"She had been in on the hunt for Nusair from the beginning. We all have, and we want to see it through."

Claire could understand that. "What was her name?"

"Deidre Howard." Grave lines marred his handsome face as he said the name, allowing Claire to see just a little of what his decision to keep Deidre on his team had cost him.

As frustrated as Claire was just now with the whole Nusair situation, part of her wanted to reach out to Krueger. To comfort him for a loss for which he clearly still felt responsible.

Oh, yes, they were very, very much alike.

"So getting Nusair is personal for you." Claire wasn't sure that was a good thing.

He pushed back the sides of his jacket and slid his hands into his pockets. "Do you doubt my objectivity where Nusair is concerned?" His guard had slipped a little now, giving her another glimpse of how badly he wanted her to believe in him. Maybe almost as badly as she needed to.

"Yes." She didn't see any point in lying to him. "But I've also seen you in action. I don't think you'll let it get in your way. Unfortunately I can't say the same thing for myself. I want to watch him die."

It sounded strange to her to be making such a heartless statement. But it was the way she felt. Nusair didn't deserve to live. He had killed countless people for no good reason. There were many things he could have done in support of his cause, none of which involved murder.

A hint of a smile twitched Krueger's lips. "You're one tough woman, Claire. I like that."

She shrugged. "What can I say? He backed me against a wall."

He moved closer. "I can't let you just walk into a trap. Not again." His voice was softer, but no less determined.

Oh, she got it now. So this was why everyone else had disappeared. Evidently a showdown was planned.

"It's my choice, Krueger. Not yours. This isn't like five years ago."

His hands slipped out of his pockets and braced

at his waist. She recognized the move, an effort to keep his hands to himself.

"But the result will be the same," he challenged. "And this is my operation. I can't let you do this. We've taken too many risks already."

His concern touched her, but she understood what he already knew no matter how he painted it. Nusair would not stop. She moved her head side to side. "I won't let another child go through what I watched Joey and Chad endure. I don't want to wait two hours. I don't want to wait at all. I want to do this. Now."

"We're going to offer an exchange."

Worry drew her brow into a frown. "What kind of exchange?"

"I'm going to offer Kaibar in exchange for your clemency."

That was crazy. "You're going to let your prisoner go? The number-two guy on the list?" She couldn't believe what she had just heard. "I thought we didn't negotiate with terrorists." She was pretty sure even a guy like Krueger didn't have the power to make that decision.

His lips quirked a half smile, which didn't reach his eyes. "I didn't say I was going to let him go. I said I was going to *offer* an exchange. I'm hoping this will buy us some time. Maybe even draw Nusair out into the open."

"You might distract him for a day but you know that's not going to solve the situation." What was he thinking? Even she could see the holes in that strategy. Maybe she was too tired. She couldn't follow this, couldn't hope to read him. The one thing she knew with complete certainty was that he wanted to protect her.

"By then it'll be too late."

She frowned. "What do you mean, it'll be too late? Too late for what?"

"You'll be dead."

Now that gave her pause. "I'm afraid I don't follow what you mean."

His hands dropped to his sides. He was losing the battle on keeping them to himself. "If you're dead, Nusair can't seek his revenge. So, we'll make you dead."

"You mean like witness protection?" This sounded less and less appealing all the time.

He reached for her hand, held on to her fingers with his own. "Yes. Nusair's attempts at revenge will end and you can go on with your life." That glimmer of desperation was back. He'd come up with this plan to save her. A last ditch effort to keep her alive.

"Only with another name and in a new location." Been there, done that. She'd already given up one life. Losing another was not what she'd had in mind.

On the other hand, losing her life was exactly what she'd resigned herself to. Only she had assumed she would actually be dead.

"I don't think so." She tugged her hand free of his, couldn't let him use that connection to sway her. God knew she needed someone to lean on right now, but she couldn't let him persuade her to change her mind that way.

"It will be difficult at first," Krueger admitted, "but you'll adjust. You've already severed any ties with your only family. I know you have friends here, but I believe this is the best solution."

Wow. He was serious. No wonder everyone had disappeared. She wasn't expected to be happy about this. Was anyone ever happy about such an offer?

She wanted to say she'd have to think about it, but there was no time. Another child could already have been targeted.

A knock on the door preceded Talkington's entrance from the hall outside the suite. "I'm sorry to interrupt, sir, but there's an urgent call for Miss Grant."

Nusair?

Fear slid like ice through her veins.

Not yet…it was too soon.

Please let it be too soon.

"I assume this isn't Nusair," Krueger proposed.

"No, sir, it's Miss Vernon."

Claire relaxed marginally. "Is she all right?" Any relief she'd experienced evaporated as she recalled that he'd said the call was urgent.

"She's fine, ma'am," Talkington said to Claire. "She's at school and she says she needs to speak with you right away."

Krueger nodded. "Put the call through to the room."

Talkington, via his communications link, told Nance to put through the call.

Claire walked over to the phone on the desk and reached for the receiver the instant it rang. Krueger picked up the other extension on the table near the sofa. He gave Claire a nod to go ahead.

"Darlene?"

"Claire, I'm glad I could get through to you."

"What's wrong? Are the children okay?"

"It's not the children."

Something in her friend's voice told Claire to brace herself. "Just tell me what it is, Darlene. What's happened?"

"It's your sister…she's here. She didn't know how to find you so she came to the school. She said she saw the school on the news."

Claire couldn't respond to the news. She didn't know what to say.

"Claire, she wants to see you. I told her I'd call. She's waiting in the vice principal's office."

"Miss Vernon, this is Special Agent Krueger."

Claire, still too stunned to speak, listened and watched as Krueger took charge of the situation.

"Tell Ms. Stewart that I'll send two of my agents to the school to pick her up. They should be there in twenty minutes." Krueger gave Talkington a hand signal only the two of them understood and Talkington rushed out of the room.

"Okay," Darlene said hesitantly. "I'll let her know."

Krueger placed the receiver he held back into its cradle. Darlene, having heard the click and, obviously, assuming the call had ended, hung up as well. Claire stood there, the receiver still clutched in her hand.

Her sister was here. In Seattle. She wanted to see Claire.

Krueger walked toward her, his gaze steady on hers, a mixture of resignation and determination simmering there.

Anger or maybe confusion catapulted through her. "Why did you do that?" She slammed the receiver back onto the base. "How do you know I want to see my sister?"

He kept coming. "Her name is Whitney Stewart now. She remarried about three years ago."

Claire blinked. How could he know that? She…

What was she saying? He was FBI. He could find out anything.

"Her daughter's name is Christina Gail, after you and your mother," he added gently as he moved in toe-to-toe with her.

She wasn't Christina anymore. She'd changed her name to Claire years ago.

"My sister hates me," she said, her voice quavering in spite of all her efforts.

"Her name is Whitney," Krueger reminded, as if she didn't know her own sister's name. He touched her arm, let his hand slide down until his fingers entwined with hers once more.

"I know her name." She should have yanked her hand free of his, but she couldn't bring herself to do it. Maybe she was just a coward pretending to be brave. Any second now she'd probably fall to pieces.

"She's here, Claire. I know you want to see her." He lifted his free hand, touched her cheek so tenderly her chest ached.

She blinked twice, three times. She hated that a stupid tear streamed down her cheek anyway. She wasn't usually such a baby. He swiped it away. She wanted desperately to lean into him, but then he'd win. He'd get his way and she'd end up doing things she didn't want to do.

"She pushed me out of her life after..." God, she couldn't say it.

"After you protected her and her daughter from her abusive husband. I know," he said gently. "She hated you at first, but she's come to terms with what happened now. She wants to see you." His fingers threaded into her hair, massaged her scalp as if he'd known somehow she needed him to touch her right there.

What was he doing to her? Claire drew away from his touch, needing to keep her head clear. "How do you know she's come to terms with anything? If she has, why didn't she let me know?"

"She didn't know how to find you. You'd changed your name. She had no idea where you were." Even though he was no longer touching her, the intensity in his eyes reached out to her, refused to let her go. "When she heard about what happened here, she still had no idea it was you until your picture was flashed all over the news."

Claire swiped at her cheeks. How did he know all this? Wait, they had been watching her sister's home. Probably monitoring everything she did and said, monitoring her phone calls for threats. Not that Claire resented what they'd done; she didn't. But this was too much. All of it. The children. Nusair. *Him.*

"There's no time for this." She couldn't handle anything else. It was too just much. Nusair could call again at any moment. The last thing she wanted was her sister anywhere even close to the line of fire.

Krueger wrapped his long fingers around her hand again. That sweet, relentless gesture tugged at every part of her that made her a woman. The urge to throw herself in his arms was an agonizing ache inside her no matter how badly she wanted to deny it.

"I'll make you a deal," he murmured as he pulled her closer still.

"The only deal I want to make is with Nusair," she argued, trying to hang on to her courage. More lies designed to cover the vulnerability she felt. She seemed to be doing a lot of lying lately. She hoped the good Lord took the circumstances into consideration when she reached the Pearly Gates…if she even got that far.

"You see your sister," Krueger said, his forehead touching hers, his lips so close, "and I'll make sure we reach a compromise on the way we do this thing with Nusair that accomplishes just what you want to make happen."

She looked up, deep into those emerald eyes. "How can you make a promise like that?" Her pulse reacted to the memory of how his kiss had swept her so far away from this ugly reality. Even the way his fingers curled around hers made her want to pretend all of it away.

His lips spread into a full-fledged smile. Nice teeth, she noted to her dismay. She was totally taken with this man. All these years she had been happy alone because she'd been certain that she deserved no better…and now she wanted so much more and it was too late.

"I still have to work out a few details, but I'm certain what I have in mind will work. You have to trust me, Claire. Can you do that?" He squeezed her hand, sending a wave of warmth in to quell the fears clawing at her. The hope in his eyes made her want to say yes.

Other than Darlene, Claire hadn't trusted anyone in a very long time. He was asking a lot.

"Okay. But don't make me regret it, Krueger. I did too much of that in the past."

He reached up with his free hand and gently touched her lips. "You won't regret it. You have my word." And then he placed a chaste kiss there. "I don't want there to be any regrets between us."

She looked deeply his eyes. "Promise me that if I make it through this, you won't just walk away and pretend you never said that, Krueger. I need to know that."

Another of those beautiful smiles claimed his lips. "There's no way I'm walking away."

Chapter 12

Thirty minutes later Claire waited alone in the parlor of the hotel suite for her sister's arrival. The initial shock had worn off but she still couldn't quite believe her sister had come.

Talkington and the other agents were working in the suite across the hall. Claire had learned that Krueger not only had this suite and the one across the hall, but he also had the rooms on either side of this one. That prevented anyone from getting close to her while she was here.

The team was reviewing surveillance tapes and tracking calls and God knows what else in an

attempt to pinpoint Nusair's location or any movement out of his people. Krueger was convinced he
was in the city. Claire had thought so as well that
morning at her demolished house. He'd spoken as
if he were watching her. Krueger had explained
that Nusair might have been watching her via a
surveillance device operated by some of his men
who were close by.

Krueger had other reasons for believing Nusair
was in Seattle. An airport facial recognition scan-
ner had locked in on an arriving passenger who
proved a thirty percent match to Nusair. The arriving passenger, Henry Vaughn, was supposedly
French and had arrived in Seattle from an airport in
Paris.

His arrival had coincided with the right time
frame. He'd landed in Seattle-Tacoma's airport,
Sea-Tac, approximately twelve hours after Habib
was killed. Sufficient time for him to have heard
the news and made travel arrangements.

Henry Vaughn had subsequently vanished.
The FBI had gotten word of his arrival too late
to track him.

They'd run a check on the name *Henry Vaughn*
and come up with a French businessman who
came to America two or three times a year for
business purposes. He'd listed connections and
contacts with several American companies, none

of which had panned out. No one admitted to knowing a Henry Vaughn.

Vaughn's travel to the U.S. during the past two years coincided with cities where known Nusair cells operated. Apparently Vaughn had been traveling in and out of major U.S. airports without notice for four years. Visual-recognition technology hadn't been in place in some airports until more recently so that may have been the reason. Still, it was hard to believe the man came and went so easily with no one noticing.

To Claire, that was the scariest part of all.

Krueger had updated her on the security at her school. Every hour the grounds and facility were searched for threats. The buses, the arriving vehicles, nothing went unsearched. The male students who were only sons were still homebound. There were twenty; each home was under FBI surveillance.

Hamid Kaibar still refused to talk. Krueger continued to believe that he would if Nusair were out of the picture. With Nusair taken out of the scenario, Kaibar would be much better off cutting a deal. Bashir Rafsanjani, who had escaped from the school the day of the attack, was still at large.

If they could just take down Nusair, the rest would fall into place.

Nusair had made no attempt to contact Claire

since the incident at Port Townsend early that morning. Three hours had passed and she hoped they still had a little more time. But she couldn't count on anything.

She needed more time.

For the first time in six years she would see her sister again. Considering what would likely come next, it might be her only opportunity.

Six years ago, Claire had been a second-year teacher at the elementary school in her hometown. Her sister had been married and eight months pregnant. Since Claire had returned from college she had recognized that something was wrong with Whitney's husband. He'd always been a jerk and she'd known it. But this was way more than that. She had him pegged as bipolar. Whitney adamantly denied the possibility. Still, the bruises and raging fights, along with his mood swings, escalated.

Claire had understood that her sister was in denial. Since their mother had passed away when Whitney was just twelve years old, Claire had been the mother in a lot of ways. As Whitney had gotten older she had resented that. Claire almost didn't go away for college, things had gotten so bad with her sister's behavior, but her father had insisted. Going away had proven to be a mistake.

When she'd learned that her sister had dropped out of school and gotten married, Claire was mortified. But it was done. Whitney resented her meddling and made her feelings quite clear. Claire had resumed her studies and tried to put the worries out of her mind.

On graduation day, her sister and father had both been there, her sister sporting a black eye behind her sunglasses, her father with two cracked ribs for stepping in the way of Tad the bully.

Claire had accepted a job at home to be close to her father and her sister, whether her sister wanted her or not. Six months later their father was dead of a heart attack. Claire had no doubt that his death had been hastened by the behavior of his youngest daughter's insane husband.

Tad Farmer was a dud of a son, a dud of a husband, and he would have been a dud of a father.

When Whitney had finally come to Claire, scared for her life, Claire had made a decision. Tad would not hurt her sister again. Whitney was all that Claire had left. She would not stand for his abuse any longer.

The district attorney had tried to turn that around and call it motivation, premeditation actually. But Claire's attorney, an old friend of the family, had known the judge for far longer than the district attorney had. Claire was certain that relationship was the only reason she hadn't faced a trial.

The charges had been dropped. Tad's death was ruled as self-defense.

Claire had gained her life but lost her sister.

A quick rap on the door announced that Nance had arrived with her sister. Claire pushed away thoughts of the past and stood. She took a deep breath and prepared for whatever happened. She assumed if her sister had come that she was worried about her…but she couldn't be certain. Maybe Whitney wanted to throw this latest incident in her face and call her a killer as she had the last time they'd seen each other.

Claire was being irrational. Her sister would not come this far to do that. No matter. She didn't want to get her hopes up and be disappointed.

There were times in the past six years that Claire had dreamed of this moment coming about in some way. She just hadn't ever really believed it would happen. She wasn't sure she believed it now.

And she definitely hadn't considered that, once it did come to be, the reunion might very well be the last time she ever saw her sister again.

She crossed the room, steeled herself once more and opened the door.

She took in the sister she hadn't laid eyes on in six long years.

Whitney had grown into a beautiful woman. She

wasn't that kid sister Claire remembered anymore. Gone were the eyebrow ring and the trashy attire. She looked amazing and smart and *mature*.

"Hello, Christina."

"Hello." Claire was sure she should say more, but her brain wouldn't string the words together. Instead, she opened the door wider for her sister to come in. She gestured to the seating area. "We can sit."

Claire didn't wait for an answer. She strode straight over to the sofa. Whitney moved a bit more hesitantly, finally choosing the chair directly across from Claire. Agent Nance closed the door, leaving them alone. It felt strange and at the same time wondrous.

"You look good, Christina." Whitney managed a shaky smile. "I mean, Claire."

For the first time since she'd made the decision, Claire regretted having changed her name. She'd done it in a moment of anger. She'd decided that if her sister wanted nothing to do with her that she might as well erase the person she used to be. Changing her last name would have been far more difficult, so she hadn't bothered. She'd calmed down by that time. So long ago. Claire had changed a lot in that time, but not nearly as much as Whitney had if her appearance were any indicator.

"Thanks." Claire managed a smile she hoped

didn't look as strained as it felt. "You look great." She moved her shoulders up and then down in surprise. "You're all grown up."

Whitney reached into her purse and pulled out a small photo album. "I thought you might want to see pictures of Christie." She looked down at the album in her hand, traced the scrolling flowers that framed the words Precious Moments. "I named her after you."

Claire's heart started that insistent pounding and her eyes burned as if she'd gotten shampoo in them. "That's very flattering." She held out her hand and her sister placed the album there. Claire held it a moment, reluctant to open it. The notion was foolish, but she was so afraid that the wrong word or move would somehow turn back the clock to that last time they'd seen each other. The ugly words echoed even now in Claire's head.

She ordered her mind to stop the torment. The past was over. This was now.

"She looks like you," Whitney said as Claire flipped slowly through the photos.

"She's too gorgeous to look like me," Claire said more to herself than to her sister. The girl did have Claire's wild mane. But then Whitney had a little of that, too. But there was her nose...her niece had Claire's nose for sure. The smile did look a little familiar, she admitted.

"She's so much like you," Whitney pressed. "She even talks like you. It's uncanny. I catch myself saying her name and thinking I'm talking to you."

Claire reached the last photo, traced the precious face there, then closed the album and handed it back to her sister. "I know you're very proud of her."

Whitney nodded. She held out her left hand and showed off her ring. "I got married again." Her eyes glittered with unshed tears but there was joy in her words. "Reggie Stewart. He's so good to me, Chri—Claire. You just wouldn't believe how much he loves Christie. We have this beautiful house and I get to stay home with my daughter."

Claire was glad. "That's great." All those times she'd dreamed of this moment, she hadn't expected it to hurt this badly. Just sitting here looking at her sister, listening to her talk about her daughter and their life, was tearing Claire apart inside.

She'd missed all of it. None of it included her. It never would.

Whitney carefully placed the album back in her purse. She clasped her hands in her lap then and stared at them for a long moment. The red highlights in her dark hair complemented her porcelain complexion. She looked phenomenal in the royal-blue dress. She looked happy.

"When I heard," Whitney began, her voice shook this time, "about the situation at the school and how you'd risked your life for that child, I knew…" She pressed her hands to her face for a moment in an effort to hold back the tears glittering in her eyes. "I knew," she cried, "that you'd saved that child just like you saved me." A sob choked out of her with the last.

Claire felt her own tears brim. Tissues. There had to be some around here somewhere. She got up, her movements mechanical, and went to the desk for the box there. The tissues would help. Once they'd calmed down everything would be fine. When she turned around Whitney was out of her chair and coming toward her.

"I was wrong," she said raggedly. "You did what you did to save my life. To save my child's life and I didn't see that back then." She trembled with the force of her emotions. "I was young and selfish and stupid. I was wrong."

Claire offered her a tissue. Whitney didn't seem to notice; her gaze was fixed on Claire's.

"Can you forgive me, Christina…Claire?"

Claire placed the box of tissues back on the desk. This part she knew. She'd thought about this for a long time.

She leveled her bleary gaze on her sister's. "There's nothing to forgive, Whitney." It was the first time she'd spoken her sister's name in years. "You did what you thought you had to do and so did I. Holding a grudge wouldn't change what happened. You don't need my forgiveness for the decision you made."

Fighting back the growing sobs, Whitney shook her head and reached for Claire's hands. "No. I was wrong. I shut you out of my life when I wouldn't have had a life if you hadn't stepped in and protected me the way you did. I made a mistake."

Claire's knees were a little wobbly. She had wanted to hear those words for so long and now that she had she was scared to death that somehow she'd misunderstood. That she would finally believe the ugly past was over and then find out it wasn't.

"You killed that sorry son of a bitch and he deserved to die." The passion behind those words startled Claire. "You gave up everything to make me happy and I was too stupid to appreciate any of it. Let me make that right, Claire. Let's not let the past stand between us anymore. I love you. You're my sister. I want you back in my life."

But it was too late.

Claire held the words inside her. How could fate be so cruel? She finally had her sister back and now she had to go away…she had to die in order to stay alive. Was it really worth it?

Having her sister back was worth the world… even if for only a moment.

Whatever happened an hour from now, they had this minute. Claire threw her arms around her sister and held her close. "I've missed you."

For a long time they stood there just like that, holding each other and crying. Then they wiped their eyes and talked and laughed about silly, insignificant things. And it was like it used to be…before the ugliness.

All too soon there was another knock on the door. Krueger didn't wait for an invitation.

"Ladies, I'm sorry to cut your visit short, but we can't put this off any longer."

Fear gripped Claire. "He hasn't taken another child, has he?"

"No. There's been no movement, but we have to initiate preventive protocol *now*."

This was it.

He didn't have to spell it out.

When she walked out this door she wouldn't be coming back. She wouldn't see her sister again.

Claire turned back to Whitney. "I'm sorry we don't have more time." She took her sister's hands. "Darlene, my friend you met at school, has something for you." The urge to cry all over again almost stole her newly gained composure.

Whitney's face turned worried. "Where are

you going?" She glanced at Krueger. "What's happening now?"

Claire squeezed her hands. "There's something I have to do. Don't worry about me."

"We'll talk again later?"

The hope in her sister's eyes was almost Claire's undoing. She hugged Whitney again. "I have lots to tell you." She drew back and looked in her eyes. "I love you. Please know that I have never *not* loved you, even for a second."

"Ms. Stewart, Agent Nance will escort you to another suite. You'll be provided with full-time security while you're in Seattle."

Claire let her sister go. "Don't worry," she assured her when Whitney still looked hesitant.

Agent Nance escorted Whitney from the suite and closed the door.

"Give me a second." Claire grabbed some tissues from the desk and took care of her damp cheeks and runny nose. When she'd composed herself as best she could she turned back to Krueger. "What's going on?"

"I have a plan."

The anticipation in his eyes was contagious.

"I hope this is good."

He threaded his fingers into her hair and pulled her close but he didn't kiss her as she would have liked him to. "It's good."

But would it be good enough to fool a terrorist like Nusair?

Claire took a deep breath. "So let's do it."

A big, shiny black commercial-sized van waited in the parking lot outside the Plaza.

"All you have to do," Krueger reminded, "is get in the van and we'll get you to safety."

She nodded. "You'll make sure my sister is protected?"

"I'll be with your sister."

She drew in a shaky breath. "You're sure this is the best way to do this? Nothing can go wrong?"

"This is the best way. Nothing will go wrong. Your location was leaked to the press and we've got to get you moved before Nusair can get someone in here to attempt a hit."

It seemed impossible that the reunion with her sister had taken place barely a half hour ago and now she had to go. It just wasn't fair.

"Okay."

"Wait."

Confused, she looked up at him. He'd been rushing her to get a move on and now he told her to wait?

He grabbed her by the shoulders and kissed her hard on the lips with God and all of his agents watching. He kissed her thoroughly. Kissed her the way a man should kiss a woman. In her entire thirty years she had never been kissed like this. She could kiss him like this forever.

"Go," he murmured against her lips before pulling completely away, "Talkington and Holman will be right there with you."

Why couldn't she have met him any other time? Any other place? Under different circumstances?

Still a little dazed, Claire left the hotel lobby, an agent on either side of her. Outside there were another dozen or so agents forming a long line between the entrance and the area of the parking lot where the van waited. Off to the right, being held behind barricades by the Seattle Police, were dozens of television reporters, cameras rolling. Claire had the spotlight. The whole country would be watching. And all she wanted was her life back. But that wasn't going to happen. The next few moments would ensure that fate.

When they reached the van, Agent Holman skirted the hood and climbed into the driver's seat. The windows were tinted so dark she could scarcely make out his image. Agent Talkington opened the rear passenger's door and Claire climbed in. Talkington climbed in next to her.

Ten seconds later the engine cranked and the van exploded.

Debris flew for hundreds of yards. People

around the hotel screamed and ran for cover. The agents who had been lined up outside the hotel rushed around and attempted to control the panic. Two of them converged on the flaming vehicle and tried to look inside but there would be no way to attempt a rescue.

Heat from the flames made Claire dizzy, but she was unhurt. She only wished she'd opted not to wear this sweater.

Having scrambled out of the van and retreated behind the blast shield according to plan, she and Agents Talkington and Holman hovered, trying to make themselves as small as possible. The small blast shield, much smaller than the one used at the mall, had been set up only about three yards from the van's driver's side. A grouping of trees and shrubs provided cover behind the shield. The reporters and television cameras were on the other side of the van some two hundred feet away. The agents on the ground would keep anyone from coming near the location of the blast.

Thank God the whole thing, so far, had worked as planned. The idea of climbing into a vehicle destined for an explosion was definitely not something she wanted to do again anytime soon.

Talkington was saying something but Claire couldn't hear him. Then she remembered the earplugs. She pulled them out and dropped them into her pocket.

"What?"

"Get ready."

Claire heard the squeal of tires before the vehicles came into view. SWAT. A large black panel truck and two black vans similar to the one that had exploded barreled into the parking lot. A fire truck arrived right behind them. Once the flames were doused, the SWAT vehicles moved in closer.

Local channel news helicopters were already coming. She could hear the whop-whop of their propellers.

"Move!" Talkington urged. "We have to move before the copters are overhead!"

The blast shield was military green to blend in with the landscape behind them. Their location in the parking lot had been carefully selected down to the last blade of grass for this staged performance.

Claire and the two agents slipped into the side doors of another waiting van that had been parked so near the shrubs and trees that branches literally poked into the vehicle's interior.

Once they were settled in the rear cargo area, Claire took her first deep breath.

"You're sure," she asked as an afterthought, "that it won't blow up again like in the movies?"

Holman shook his head. "We drained the fuel

tank. There was barely enough gas to start the engine."

That sounded reasonable.

"Now we wait," Talkington reminded. "The driver of this vehicle is one of our agents. He'll take us to the location of the next phase of the operation as soon as things are under control here. If he tries to leave any sooner it would look suspicious."

The next phase of the operation.

That was where things got tricky.

Claire's entire future depended upon how Nusair responded to this setup. The press would be leaked information indicating that Abdul Nusair had made good on his threats to avenge his son's death.

The world would believe that Claire was dead.

Including her sister and her friends.

That was the only part she felt bad about in all this. The people who cared about her would grieve her death. She hated to trick them this way, but it was her only option. If she didn't go this route she was dead anyway.

Nusair would not stop until he knew for an absolute certainty that she was dead.

In fact, she and Krueger were counting on exactly that.

Chapter 13

The county morgue.

That was the location of the next phase of the operation.

The FBI had taken control of all but a small section of the facility's ongoing operations. One of the refrigerated storage rooms, a cadaver room, was the primary part of the strategy.

Three bodies, all disfigured to some degree and with features like hair color, height and weight that resembled Claire and the two agents who'd supposedly died in the blast with her, had been borrowed and tagged for the show to come. More than a dozen FBI agents were posing as morgue personnel for the next few hours.

The plan was to lure Nusair here and then take him down. Seemed simple enough, but it was an unprecented operation, according to Krueger.

At first the idea that Nusair would attempt to view her body firsthand, to ensure she was indeed dead, had made her skeptical, but the more she thought about it the more she decided Krueger might have a point. Nusair would want proof that she was really dead. He would want to see with his own eyes.

The news reports would not be enough. He was not a man who left loose ends or anything to chance.

Krueger had taken over one of the medical examiner's offices across the hall from the refrigerated storeroom. Surveillance had been put in place that allowed him to watch the corridor outside and the storage room from a monitor installed in the borrowed office. In addition, agents were posted in the parking lot and around the building to watch for Nusair's arrival. Agents Talkington and Holman monitored the main corridor leading to this wing of the facility from yet another office farther down the hall. If anyone came near the storage room where the bodies were kept, they would know about it in real time.

The agents, some wearing white lab coats, were

heavily armed. Watching the preparations, one would have thought the men and women were preparing to go to war, not just stop one demented man and his small band of followers.

But this was, in fact, a war. And Nusair was slick. Far too slippery to take any chances.

Claire looked around the office. Medical journals lined the bookshelves on one wall. Next to the locked door was a credenza-style cabinet that now held the monitor allowing Krueger to observe the video feed from the corridor as well as the storage room. Additional stacks of medical journals had been moved to the floor in the corner temporarily.

A large wooden desk claimed a significant portion of the available floor space. Another credenza stood against the wall behind the desk. This credenza served as a holding place for what looked like hundreds of loose files. It looked as if the medical examiner was seriously behind in his paperwork.

In contrast, the desk was neat and clear with nothing more than a lamp and a name plate on its polished surface. Claire had claimed the generously sized leather executive chair behind the desk in hopes of staying out of Krueger's way. He hadn't been happy about her insistence on staying involved, but she wasn't about to be hidden away while this thing went down.

She wanted to be here. She wanted to know for sure that Nusair would come. Maybe she had no control over the situation but some part of her stuck by the idea that her presence would draw him. He wanted the woman who had killed his son. She needed to be here if for no other reason than for stacking the odds. It was a matter of simple physics, as long as she was here she couldn't be anywhere else. On some level she believed he had already sensed her determination to be involved as completely as possible.

She'd been here less than an hour and already she could tell this was going to be a long evening, maybe an even longer night. Who knew if Nusair would even show. If he didn't, her life as she knew it would be on permanent sabbatical. That was the part she didn't want to see happen. Unfortunately that component was also well out of her sphere of control.

Everything from this point forward depended upon Nusair's reaction to today's staged production in the hotel parking lot. He would, of course, know *he* hadn't blown up the van, but he couldn't discount the possibility that some of his followers might have. There was no way to prove the explosion was rigged without verifying her death.

At least she hoped it worked so logically.

Krueger settled on the edge of the neat desk,

drawing her attention to him. Not necessarily a good thing considering she'd been closed up *alone* in this room with him for almost an hour. Dwelling on this little attraction brewing between them was such a lost cause. Her life was either over or it wasn't. Whatever the case, Krueger would move on with his.

But he had promised not to walk away. As much as she feared she shouldn't, she hung on to that hope.

"Tell me what happened between you and your sister."

The sound of his deep voice made her edgier than she already was. Her emotions were already raw. Delving into that subject matter wouldn't help.

"You know what happened. You have a file on me, remember?" He'd recited lines and lines from the reports within that file.

He stood, took off his jacket and placed it on the chair in front of the desk. Claire watched every little move with far too much interest.

"I know the facts, nothing more."

She didn't really want to talk about her sister right now. The reunion still felt surreal...the idea that Whitney had wanted to make things right a long time ago had thrown Claire into a whole other turmoil. She hadn't processed what it all meant yet.

However, Krueger wasn't the kind of man to allow his questions to be played off without a battle. And, truthfully, any kind of distraction might be a good idea right now.

"Our mother died when I was eighteen, Whitney was twelve. Our father worked long hours at the manufacturing plant to support us. I had no choice but to step up to the plate and be the mother. We tried to get through the grief, but my sister didn't handle the loss well."

For a few seconds Claire got lost in the painful memories. Krueger didn't push.

"She did all the typical rebellious teenage stuff and more," Claire went on eventually. "After I left for college things got worse. She dropped out of high school, ran off and married a local jerk."

Krueger's gaze was sympathetic. "I'm sure that was tough on your father."

Claire nodded, her own guilt still as heavy as ever. It never went away. "I should have been there, but my father insisted that I go on to college."

"You did the right thing. If you'd stayed it might not have made any difference."

"But it might have," she countered. "We'll never know." That was the hardest part.

When he didn't say more she figured he'd heard all he needed to. Most of the rest of the story was probably in the file.

"You were there when she needed you most,"

he said softly. That he cared enough to say so meant more than it should have to her.

"I did what I had to do." She had. The doubt was gone. And that made all the difference.

"Seeing your sister today was important," Krueger acknowledged. "I'm glad she came."

For a woman who was dead, Claire suddenly felt as if she had plenty to live for. Definitely something to smile about. "Me, too."

The possibility that it might be the last time she saw her sister diminished the moment considerably. "If he doesn't show, what next?" She had a vague idea, but Krueger hadn't gone into detail and she hadn't asked. Maybe she should now. Then again, knowing might jinx her.

She didn't care. She needed to know.

He loosened his ever-present tie, making her wish those hands were touching her the way they had that first time he kissed her. Stop it, she ordered.

"If Nusair doesn't show then Claire Grant has no choice but to stay dead. The only way to ensure he doesn't come after you or the people you care about again is for him to believe that you're dead."

"So I'll go into witness protection." It wasn't a question. She understood that her options were limited, nonexistent actually, beyond the idea of catching Nusair. As long as he was free, she would be a prisoner in many respects.

"It's not such a bad thing considering," he offered.

"I guess not." In a way, he was right. She was lucky to be alive. As unfair as this whole thing was, bad things happened to good people every day. She needed to keep that in mind and remember to count her blessings.

Krueger hadn't allowed her to watch the news. He knew it would be too painful. She could just imagine what Whitney and Darlene were going through.

And her students.

"Don't go there, Claire."

She looked up. Krueger was assessing her emotional state all too well without her having to say a word.

"I regret the fallout for the kids."

Krueger leaned forward, covered her hand with his. "If all teachers were like you the world would be a far better place."

"It's a question of basic human compassion, Krueger. I'm no saint looking for martyrdom." Any teacher would have felt the same way. She wasn't a hero. She was just a woman who'd done what she had to do.

If she were so special she wouldn't be sitting here feeling sorry for herself because she couldn't have her life back. Unfortunately she was far too human.

"You see," he tossed right back at her, "I rest my case. I've worked with my share of those headed for witness protection, trust me, you rise well above the usual suspect."

Amused and undeniably flattered, she adopted a skeptical expression. "I'm not so sure that was a compliment. Aren't a lot of the folks in the program former criminals?"

He tugged at her hand until she scooted up on the desk next to him. He turned his head so that he was looking at her with only a few inches between them. "We're not going to assume the worst. This isn't over, Claire."

"So what do we do now?"

He leaned closer, brushed his lips against hers. "This isn't standard procedure," he murmured, the feel of his lips vibrating against hers making her shiver. "I don't usually break the rules."

That she could believe.

He kissed her slowly, tenderly and she wanted it to be more. She moved her hands to his chest and relished all that he could offer her even if it was only a kiss.

He drew away, his breath ragged, his eyes full of the same yearning she felt. When he reached into the pocket of his trousers and removed his ringing cell phone, she knew the moment was over.

"Krueger."

A wave of anticipation washed over her. She tried not to fear the worst as he'd said, but it was difficult not to. She wanted this over, no more casualties, no matter the price to her.

Maybe that was the mark of a martyr, but she didn't see it that way. No more children were going to be risked to satisfy a raging lunatic on account of her. She was willing to die to stop Nusair. That wasn't being a hero, that was simply being a decent human being.

The sudden shift in the tone of Krueger's voice hauled her attention to his end of the evidently tense conversation. He stood, his back to her, his free hand rubbing the back of his neck.

"Continue the evacuation, but nobody makes a move until I'm on site, understand? Not a single move." Pause. "I'm on my way."

He snapped the phone closed, grabbed his jacket and pulled it on before stuffing the phone into his pocket. "We have to relocate."

Something was wrong.

Claire was on her feet before her brain had even issued the order. "What's going on? Why're we moving?"

His face was grim.

"Apparently Nusair suspected we'd set him up. His people zeroed in on the hotel rather than the trap we'd laid."

"The hotel?" At first the significance didn't register. Then it did. "He has my sister?"

"I'm afraid so. If you aren't there in forty-five minutes, he's going to kill her."

The twenty-five minutes it took to reach the hotel were the most tension-filled of Claire's life. She had thought nothing could ever top what she'd gone through getting to those children, but this did. She wanted to crawl into a hole and die.

This was way past enough.

The area of the parking lot where the explosion had occurred was still cordoned off. Hundreds of guests had been ushered to the far side of the undamaged parking area to the west of the main entrance. The Seattle police were in place overseeing crowd control.

Several men she recognized as FBI agents were working outside a van parked beneath the dropoff and pick-up portico at the hotel's main entrance. As her SUV neared the group, she recognized the setup. This was the base of operations.

Her heart rate accelerated, sending adrenaline through her veins, along with no small amount of panic.

"Bring me up to speed," Krueger ordered as they reached Agent Carver.

Claire remembered him from the first day she'd been brought in by the FBI.

"He's on the fourteenth floor. The four agents we had guarding Mrs. Stewart are down."

"Damn." Krueger slammed his fist against the side of the van. "All dead?"

"Only one dead, the rest are still alive but we can't get to them to assess their condition."

Not only did her sister's life depend upon her, Claire realized, the lives of those agents did as well.

"Where do I need to go?" Claire stepped into the fray. "He's waiting for me, right? Where?"

Carver and Krueger exchanged a look.

"Don't start with that," she warned. "We all know what I have to do, now give me the location."

"Nusair and approximately six of his men are up there, Claire," Krueger explained, his expression graver now than before. "If we send you in, we can't protect you. My men are down."

"I don't care." This was it. She had known this moment might come. Before Krueger had come up with this latest plan she had been fully prepared to surrender to Nusair. She was prepared now. "I'm going in."

"Wait." Krueger took her arm when she headed for the entrance. "We need to rig you with communications first. At least that way we can monitor what's going on."

What she saw in his eyes wasn't at all professional. The desperation was as painful to look at as her own was to endure. She relented. At least one of them was thinking rationally. "Okay."

Krueger waved someone from the van over and an agent she didn't recognize hurried to do his bidding. He placed the necessary earpiece and tagged her with an undetectable listening device. He called it a microfiber job. It's clear color made it invisible against her navy sweater.

"Thanks." She touched the earpiece as the agent's test call sounded in her ear. "I can hear you fine," she told him.

"Excellent." He looked from her to Krueger and back. "You don't need to worry, Miss Grant, the imbedded team already has sound as well as visual, but this will take care of you if you're taken to a different location. There's a new technology tracking device built into the micro—"

"That's all Miss Grant needs," Krueger cut in.

Krueger's hand was suddenly at the small of her back ushering her toward the entrance. "This is as far as I can go with you, Claire. They're watching the lobby. Explosives are rigged for detonation if anyone other than you comes inside. The room is 1420, just down the hall from the suite of rooms we've been using for a command post."

Claire stopped and turned to face him. "What

was he talking about, the imbedded team? Did he mean the agents who are down?" He hadn't sounded as though that was what he meant.

"That's nothing you need to worry about."

Something was missing here.

"Twelve minutes remaining since the warning call," Carver announced.

Claire knew she had to go, but she wanted the whole story here. Something was wrong and Krueger's guard was firmly back in place, shielding whatever was on his mind.

"I'm not going in until I know what that means. You said your men inside were down. That agent—" she nodded toward the one who had rigged her "—just talked about the imbedded team inside. What's going on, Krueger?"

"Probability statistics showed that there was a major risk that Nusair wouldn't buy the bombing scenario. So we leaked information about your sister's location."

Disbelief and shock hit her with the impact of a launched rocket. She couldn't have heard right. "You purposely put my sister's life in danger?"

"It's not that simple—"

She slapped him as hard as she could. "Damn you, Krueger. If she dies I'm going to kick Nusair's ass and then I'm going to come back down here and kick yours."

For a moment he just stood there staring at her and then he grabbed her, held her close against his chest. She tried to pull away, but he was far too strong. What the hell did he think he was doing?

"Your sister is safe. An agent is posing as her," he whispered against her ear. "Trust me, Claire. We know what we're doing, but no one else needs to know."

His grip loosened and she drew back. His jaw was red where she'd popped him. "Okay. Maybe I won't have to kick your ass."

Krueger's guard fell away and this time she saw the fear mingled with the desperation. "Be careful in there."

"Ten minutes," Carver reminded.

Claire held Krueger's gaze a moment longer. There was a lot she would have liked to say to him, but there wasn't time. She turned away and entered the hotel.

The elegant lobby was empty, the silence deafening.

She walked to the elevators and pressed the call button. Nothing blew up. No shots were fired. Thank God.

"We have movement."

Claire didn't recognize the voice coming across her communications link. Evidently one of the agents imbedded on the fourteenth floor. Whatever that meant.

"Can you confirm that the intruder is the target?" Krueger.

A soft ding announced the arrival of the elevator. As she boarded she wondered if the target meant Nusair. Had to, she decided. She selected the fourteenth floor and leaned against the wall as the elevator doors closed.

"Negative. Male, approximately six feet, medium build, wearing sunglasses and a baseball cap."

Krueger swore.

"Intruder is entering hot zone."

Claire felt her pulse pounding. Her sister was safe but the life of those agents depended on her. She had to do this right. No mistakes. Full cooperation.

The elevator abruptly stopped. Claire checked the floor. Twelve. She glanced at the control panel. She hadn't pushed the wrong button. Fourteen was still lit.

The sound of gunfire erupted in her earpiece. Fear rose in her chest.

"We have eliminated the intruder!"

"Confirm!" Krueger fairly shouted.

The elevator doors began to glide open but the ruckus in her earpiece held most of Claire's attention. She jabbed at the button for the fourteenth floor. What was going on up there?

"Negative. I repeat, negative on the target. The downed intruder is not the target."

What did that mean? Was she supposed to continue toward the fourteenth floor? She hadn't received orders otherwise.

The elevator door started to close again.

Finally. She didn't get why they had opened unless Krueger's people were in control of their operation and the stop had been to slow her arrival since gunfire had erupted.

"Claire! Get out of there!"

Krueger's voice.

She started to ask what he meant when, at the last possible second, a hand cut between the two doors and stopped them from closing.

Her heart lunged into her throat.

"Claire! Get out of there now!"

Krueger's words rang in her ear once more but it was too late. The muzzle of a weapon had already been jammed against her forehead.

The man grabbed her by the arm with his left hand and dragged her out of the elevator.

She strained to get a better look at him. His face was not hidden by a mask as had been the case with the men who had stormed the school.

Was this Nusair? Or one of his henchmen?

The doors of the other elevator opened and he hauled her inside. He pressed the button for the top floor. With the gun jammed into her forehead, he used a handheld device to scan her body.

She realized he was looking for bugs.

Seconds later he had pinpointed the microfiber job on her sweater. He removed it and pressed it on to the elevator wall. Then he took her earpiece and tucked it into his own ear.

As he went about his business she studied his face, attempted to visualize Habib's face next to his. Same nose. Same mouth and eyes. This was Nusair all right. The resemblance was irrefutable. She'd seen the photos Krueger had of him but they were all of a man wearing one kind of camouflage or another. Either sunglasses or the traditional headgear of his homeland. None had shown a full front-on image of his face.

But this was him.

She should be screaming.... She should be scared to death. But somehow she was grateful this moment had finally arrived.

He held his finger to his lips and nudged her with the weapon. She got it. No talking until they were off the elevator.

Once they had exited onto the top floor, he hurried toward the east end of the corridor.

"You won't get away." It wasn't exactly original

but she wanted him to know. Krueger's people would get him this time.

"Perhaps not." He glanced at her, a look of indifference on his face. "But neither will you, Claire Grant."

Definitely Nusair. The sound of his voice made her tremble despite how hard she tried not to react.

When they reached the stairwell exit, instead of going down, they went up.

The roof.

Oh, boy. She was pretty sure she'd rather be shot than take a dive off a building this size. Or any building for that matter. Maybe once they got up there, if she resisted he'd simply do the easy thing and shoot her.

When they reached the roof exit the door was locked.

Thank God.

Just when she thought there might be hope, he produced a key card and opened the door.

The sound of running footsteps echoed from many floors below.

She smiled at Nusair. "They're coming for you."

Antagonizing him wasn't a good idea, but she couldn't help the dig. She might be about to die but he wasn't getting out of this one. No two ways about that.

They burst out onto the roof. The wind whipped around her. She blinked, pushed the hair out of her face and blinked again.

She'd thought it might be her eyes playing tricks on her, but now she heard it as well.

A helicopter coming…directly at them.

Chapter 14

Claire understood with complete certainty that if Nusair got her on that helicopter, when it landed, that she was finished.

She might be dead anyway, but at least here she could die on her terms. And just maybe she could buy enough time to ensure Krueger's people got Nusair. At least then her death wouldn't be for nothing.

With all her might she jerked at his hold.

He jammed the weapon harder against her skull. "Do you wish to die now, Claire Grant?"

She dug in her heels and slowed down his forward momentum. "Why not!"

"Very well, Teacher. On your knees!"

He shoved her downward.

She landed hard but never took her gaze off his. "You're a coward, Abdul Nusair. Just like your son."

Nusair's face twisted in anger.

The bullet exploded in the air.

Nusair stiffened. Surprise claimed his face.

Claire's gaze shifted from the hole in his forehead to his fingers still clutched around his weapon.

A second shot entered his chest and he staggered back.

This time Claire had the sense to scramble away from his line of fire.

Gunfire erupted from the helicopter.

Claire crouched behind a turbine roof vent. Her heart felt as if it had stopped beating altogether.

She closed her eyes and prayed none of the ricocheting bullets would hit her since there was no place else she could hide.

The whop-whop of the helicopter begun to fade and she dared to open her eyes. The helicopter swayed precariously then dropped suddenly.

"Are you hit?"

Krueger.

She looked up at him standing over her and shook her head, uncertain of her voice at this point.

He rushed over to Nusair and checked to make sure the scumbag was dead.

Several of Krueger's agents had moved to the edge of the roof. She heard one of the men say that the helicopter had made a hard landing in the parking lot. Whoever was on the helicopter wouldn't be getting away. They were surrounded.

She was glad.

Claire stood on shaky legs. She took a deep breath and walked over to where Krueger was going through Nusair's personal effects. Among his things was a picture. Claire crouched down and looked at it. Habib, his son.

Maybe the man was human after all.

"Don't go there," Krueger warned, evidently reading her mind. He was pretty good at that. "This guy doesn't deserve your remorse or your pity."

"You're right." The announcement surprised her almost as much as it apparently did him. "He was an animal."

She was glad the nightmare was finally over. Her gaze settled on Krueger once more. She was still a little ticked at him for leaving her in the dark about this part of his operation.

"Where's my sister?"

"This isn't the way this was supposed to play out," he offered, his expression revealing the depth of the regret he felt.

She felt so many things at that moment. Relief,

hope, fatigue, anger. She needed to think. To figure all this out. "Not right now, Krueger." She moved her head side to side. "Right now I just want to see my sister."

He made no attempt to hide the disappointment in his eyes. He wanted her to understand why he'd made the decisions he had. She was sure she would, later.

"I'll get you there."

Claire placed the picture of Habib next to his father and pushed to her feet.

It was really over.

Finally.

Or at least she prayed it was. If she had to worry about his followers coming after her, she couldn't deal with that right now. She was running on emotional overload.

She turned away from the scene and started walking toward the door that would lead her back into the hotel. She wanted to be as far away from here as possible.

If she lived a hundred years she never wanted to think about guns and dying again.

She would add terrorists to that list as well except that, in retrospect, she realized she couldn't watch the news and avoid any of those things.

Not everything in life was meant to be pleasant, she supposed. And staying up to snuff on current events was something she never intended to fall down on ever again.

Agent Talkington jogged up beside her. "Miss Grant, I'll take you to the safe house to see your sister."

The house was one she hadn't seen before. It reminded her of her bungalow that had been blown to bits, really old but much larger. She liked old houses.

She wondered where the FBI came up with all these different locations. Did the houses actually belong to the agency or were they borrowed?

She didn't have the energy to ask just now. She was tired. Tired and ready to move on with her life.

Her blown-up house flashed through her mind again.

She groaned. Putting her life back together would take some time.

Talkington opened her door. She snapped out of her worrisome thoughts and thanked him.

He led her up the walk. He knocked and a female agent Claire hadn't met let her in.

"This is Miss Grant," he explained. "She's here to see her sister."

Talkington didn't follow her inside. He

probably had to get back to the hotel and finish things there.

"Claire!"

Whitney hugged her so hard she couldn't breathe. When she finally let go, she surveyed Claire from head to toe and back. "I was so worried. It was bad enough when they let me believe, for about an hour, that you'd blown up in that van." She glanced at the television set that was currently showing images from the Plaza. "But when we saw that helicopter go down I was scared to death all over again."

Claire squeezed her sister's hands. "Sorry about that."

Whitney hugged her again, then said, her expression hopeful, "We have a lot to catch up on."

"Yes, we do. Let's sit."

Claire held her sister's hand as they got comfortable on the sofa. "You know they blew up my house."

"That's just terrible. You lost everything."

"Not everything." Claire thought of the photo album and the diary. She could make sure her sister got that later. "I'll be okay now that you're here."

"I was thinking," Whitney ventured, looking a little uncertain and sounding a lot nervous, "that maybe when school is out in a few weeks that you could come spend the summer with us while your house is being rebuilt."

The invitation brought tears to Claire's eyes and a leap for joy in her chest. "That would be a huge imposition on you and your family," she reminded, giving her sister a way out of the too-generous offer.

Whitney squeezed her hand. "You're part of my family, Claire. I'd like nothing better than to have you there for as long as you want to stay."

"You're sure about that?" She wanted to go so badly. To get to know Christina…to share in the happiness her sister had found.

"I'm positive."

They hugged again, until their arms were too tired to hold each other anymore.

Claire pressed a hand to her stomach. "I don't know about you, but I'm starved." She couldn't remember the last time she'd eaten.

"I can always eat," Whitney chimed in. She patted her own tummy. "Especially since I'm eating for two."

Claire's jaw dropped. "Are you pregnant?"

Whitney nodded, her eyes glittering. "Reggie and I couldn't wait to add to our family. I wanted to tell you earlier, but too much was going on. It didn't seem like the right time."

The idea sent a pang of want deep inside Claire.

Her students had always been enough to satisfy the nurturing instinct in her…. Maybe that wasn't the case anymore.

But this wasn't about Claire. This was about Whitney.

"That's wonderful, Whitney. I'm so happy for you." She hugged her sister again. Seeing her this happy was something Claire had always wanted for her younger sibling. "Momma and Daddy would be really proud of you."

Then they both cried. The agent hovering near-by cried, too. When they recovered their composure a little, Whitney introduced Claire to Agent Rebecca Neels.

Claire swiped her eyes. "We should go out and celebrate. With a huge steak."

"That sounds good."

"Sorry, ladies," Agent Neels said with visible regret, "we can't leave the house."

Claire's expression drooped as did Whitney's.

"But we can certainly have something delivered by one of my colleagues," the agent offered.

"There's just one other thing," Claire inter-jected.

Agent Neels turned an expectant gaze on Claire.

"Can your colleague pick up my friend Darlene, too? We need her to make this celebration complete."

* * *

The steak was to die for. The wine as smooth as silk, though Whitney restricted herself to juice. By the time they'd eaten their fill, Claire felt relaxed for the first time in days.

When the meal was finished, Agent Neels opted to hang out in the living room so that the ladies could have some privacy in the dining room.

Darlene poured Claire as well as herself another glass of wine. "So what's up with that Agent Krueger?"

Claire started to whistle nonchalantly. It sounded pretty pathetic. But she wasn't about to answer that question.

"Don't try that," Whitney scolded. "I saw the way he looked at you."

"And the way he touched you and the way he—"

"Enough!" Claire leaned back in her seat and glanced toward the living room. Allowing Agent Neels to overhear this conversation would not be a good thing. When she had decided it was okay to talk, Claire looked at first one and then the other seated at the table with her. "We have a little connection going on," she confessed.

"I knew it!" Darlene shouted.

"The question is," Whitney put in, "what are you going to do about it?"

Claire exhaled a heavy sigh. "I'm not sure there's anything I can do about it. He already has a significant other." Though he had promised not to walk away...that could mean many things, none of which could be what she had meant.

Two mouths formed perfect *O*s of shock.

"The job," Claire explained. "He's married to the job. I'm not sure I can compete with that. I'm not sure I even want to."

"Claire." Darlene reached for her hand. "Listen to me, friend. If the right guy comes along, you'd better fight tooth and toenail to claim him."

"You said it," Whitney confirmed. "Believe me, I've had it both ways. The wrong guy isn't worth the trouble." She smiled and her eyes took on a dreamy look. "But the right guy, he's worth the world."

Claire threw her hands up. "Okay. So I'll see what happens. Can we change the subject please?"

Darlene sipped her wine. "Maybe. Then again, he's the hottest subject I've seen lately."

"That's it." Claire stood. "I'm going to take a bath." She surveyed the naughty twosome. "I've had a tough day. I need bubble bath to take me away."

"Wait!" Whitney jumped up. "I have to go first." She pressed her hand to her still-flat belly. "This pregnancy is already keeping me running to the bathroom."

"In a house this size, surely there are two bathrooms," Darlene suggested.

"Come on." Claire gestured for her sister to follow her. "We'll check it out."

"You want to borrow something to wear?" Whitney offered as they headed for the hall.

Her sister was about the same size as Claire so she didn't see why not.

Especially considering she had a couple of blood spatters on her favorite sweater that she'd only just noticed.

"That would be great."

Whitney rounded her up a pair of jeans, panties and a pink-and-white striped blouse. Claire thanked her sister and closed herself up in the bathroom for some alone time. To everyone's relief there *were* two bathrooms, one on each end of the house, which was very good since Claire wanted to take her time and relax thoroughly. It wasn't every day a girl went up against pure evil and survived.

There was no scented oil. No bubble bath. But that was okay. She could be perfectly happy with lots of hot water. Especially since this house had the same sort of huge clawfooted tub her house had…or used to have.

Claire stared at her reflection as she pinned her hair up to keep it dry. She didn't really look any different. Despite having killed another man, having suffered three near-death experiences and having regained her sister, she looked pretty much the same.

She looked exactly like the fifth-grade teacher she'd been before all this mayhem.

Claire stripped off her clothes. She studied the bloodstains on her sweater and scowled. They wouldn't be coming out. Her gaze narrowed as she picked at something else there. Clear. Sticky. Round. The microfiber thingamajig. Hadn't Nusair stripped that off her in the elevator? Who knew? Didn't matter now. He was deader than a doornail.

Throwing the sweater aside, she stepped into the water. She leaned back in the tub and closed her eyes. Something else about the past few days was different. Her long-slumbering libido had definitely awakened.

Funny, she mused, after all these years she'd thought maybe her desire for a love life had gone into permanent retirement. To have it suddenly wake up, during all the other insanity, was totally unexpected, to say the least.

Was it possible to have one's life back after being basically dead for six long years?

Four times she'd had the hand of death brush against her in the past forty-eight hours. If she had died…she would have died without having lived at all…actually.

When she'd soothed her weary muscles long enough, she dragged herself out of the tub and dried off. She slipped on the panties and the blouse Whitney had lent her and partially buttoned it.

Now for this mass of hair. There was a blow-dryer but no straightening iron. Oh, well. She'd just have to make do. There was always a French braid. If she remembered correctly her sister had been really good at those.

The hair dryer was ancient and loud, but it worked and that was what counted. She held the dryer like a weapon in one hand and fluffed her hair with the other to help make the process go a little faster. Her thoughts took a detour and she couldn't help wondering where Krueger was now. Still rounding up those who had survived the shootout today, she supposed. Then there would be lots of reports to write. He'd been tracking Nusair for a long time. This would be a big change for Krueger.

Who would he track now? There were plenty of bad guys out there. One thing was certain, whoever Krueger set his sights on should look out. Krueger didn't give up.

Would he show up here later? He'd promised

he wouldn't just walk away. Her pulse reacted to the thought that maybe they would talk and maybe they would decide to pursue this connection. Hey, she'd survived a terrorist attack, over and over again. Anything was possible.

A cracking sound snapped her back to the here and now. Claire cocked her head and listened. There it went again. She turned the dryer off and laid it on the counter.

Another sound distracted her.

A thump.

Okay. Enough with the strange sounds. She turned around and reached for the door but the knob turned before she got there.

Claire froze.

Could be Whitney or Darlene...

The door flew open and the muzzle of a gun leveled on her face.

Her gaze traveled from the ominous end of the barrel to the hand and then to the face of the man holding the weapon.

Bashir Rafsanjani. The man who had escaped from school that day.

"I have a message for you, Claire Grant."

Terror raced through her veins. This couldn't be happening.

Where were Darlene and Whitney? Agent Neels?

An ache twisted through her. No. She wouldn't let them be dead.

"I have one for you," she fired back at him. "Your boss is dead. I watched him die just like I did his son." She was sick of being terrorized by these sons of bitches.

He backhanded her. Her head snapped back. "Stupid bitch," he snarled. "You are dead!"

She blinked away the spots floating in front of her eyes. Her face stung. "Then just do it," she challenged. "Stop your damned games and do it!"

He stepped closer, jammed the weapon against her chest; directly above her heart. "Abdul had many plans of torture for you, Claire Grant. He was a very wise man. He understood that he might not be able to finish what he started so he asked me to be prepared. If he failed I was to complete his sacred mission. He never left anything to chance. Your friend Krueger should have expected this."

She had to do something. If it were the last thing she did she would not let this man walk out of here alive.

This was over.

"You killed his only son." The man hurled the words at her. The more he talked the harder he jammed the gun into her sternum.

She kept inching away from him until the backs of her knees bumped into the tub.

Then she knew what she had to do. All she needed was an opportunity.

"His son was a coward who killed children," she challenged. "He was nothing."

He drew back his hand to slap her again. This time she sidestepped, then pivoted, throwing her weight against him. He lost his balance. She shoved him hard. He fell forward into the tub of water. Claire grabbed the hair dryer, turned it on and pitched it into the water. The twisting maneuver sent her flying backwards onto the floor. A miniexplosion made the lights blink twice before going out with a hissing pop.

Rafsanjani's body jerked and convulsed for a couple of more seconds even after the electricity had stopped flowing.

Claire scrambled to her feet. She eased a step closer to the tub and stared at the man. His eyes and mouth were open despite the fact that his head was underwater. She was pretty sure he was dead.

She had to check on the others.

She rushed into the hall and bumped square into her sister.

"Whitney! Thank God you're all right!"

"I heard the gunfire. I was in the other bathroom. I was afraid to come out until I heard you scream."

She had screamed? Claire didn't remember screaming. Maybe when she threw the dryer into the tub with that scumbag.

Darlene and Neels.

Claire rushed into the living room and her worst fears were realized. Neels was on the floor. Where the hell was Darlene?

"Call 911," she told her sister.

Neels's eyes were wide open, unblinking. She was dead. Oh, God.

"I already did," Whitney said. "I saw her like this when I rushed to find you."

Where was Darlene?

Claire rushed into the kitchen. Her friend was there. On the floor in front of the sink where she'd been cleaning up after dinner.

"No!" Claire dropped on the floor next to her. Blood had soaked the front of her blouse…but the bullet wound was below center chest.

Claire felt for a pulse. Her breath caught. It was there. Weak but there. "Whitney! We need an ambulance! Hurry!" She could hear her sister making a second call.

God, please let them hurry!

Claire put her hand over the wound and applied pressure to stop the bleeding. "Hang on for me, Darlene. Please hang on."

* * *

Claire paced the waiting room floor. Whitney had finally collapsed into a chair. But Claire couldn't sit down. She had to keep moving.

If Darlene died...she couldn't even think it.

This could not happen! She'd been in surgery for over three hours. Surely there would be some word soon.

The door to the private waiting room opened and Claire braced herself for the worst.

Krueger.

Not the doctor.

As glad as she was to see him, she couldn't help being a little disappointed.

"Hey." He walked straight up to her and put his arms around her. Some amount of relief washed over her instantly at just having him near.

"It's okay," he said softly. "I talked to the doctor just now. Darlene is doing great."

Hope welled in Claire's chest. "Are you sure?"

He nodded. "They're taking her to recovery as we speak. You'll be able to see for yourself in a couple of hours."

"Oh, thank God." Claire let go a sigh of relief.

Whitney came over and hugged her, too. "You see," she offered. "Everything's going to be fine."

Maybe. Finally.

"Good job with the blow-dryer," Krueger said teasingly, drawing her attention back to him.

Claire shrugged. "Hey, it was the only weapon I had handy."

"Maybe I should hire you for my team."

"You know," Whitney said, "I think I'll check out the menu in the cafeteria."

Her sister had to be seriously hungry to eat in a hospital cafeteria. Not to mention they'd had steak just a few hours ago.

When Whitney hesitated at the door and winked, Claire knew she was only giving her some time alone with Krueger. Wow. She didn't remember her sister being so thoughtful. Obviously she really had grown up.

When the door had closed, Claire looked deep into those green eyes. "So is this really over?"

"It's really over. Kaibar has decided to cooperate."

That was terrific news. "Do you think he might provide the locations of all the remaining cells?"

"He's already doing that. We also know that Nusair's plan was to cripple the country's major ports. What we need to confirm is whether or not his plan was a precursor to something larger. We're hoping Kaibar will help us with that. Cooperation from these people is rare. We're lucky to be getting this much."

This had to be a major coup for Krueger.

"We couldn't have gotten the job done without you, Claire. I want you to understand just how pivotal your role in this accomplishment was."

She was flattered, truly flattered. "My role was accidental, Krueger. Let's not make too much out of it."

He fell silent for a moment. Despite her determination not to, she used the time to study his handsome face. The man had a lot of terrific qualities, inside and out. Too good to be true. A legend. It took a special kind of woman to harness a legend. She wasn't so sure she was up to the task.

"I should have anticipated Rafsanjani's final move," he said, breaking the silence and settling that searching gaze on hers. "I knew better than anyone that Nusair was thorough. Hell, he had a fix on…us. He was watching us as closely as we were trying to watch him. He followed the agent who delivered the food. That mistake almost cost…"

She pressed a finger to his lips. "Stop. You're only human, Krueger." For a legend, but she kept that thought to herself.

"I promised to protect you."

They had to get past this whole regret/guilt scenario. They'd both traveled that road far too many times already. Claire ran a hand through her wild mane. She didn't even want to think about how she must look right now. "Listen, Krueger—"

"I thought you were going to call me Luke?" He captured a coiled strand of hair in his fingers and toyed with it. "I made a promise, you know. I'm not walking away." He gave her one of those crooked smiles. "I figure since we can't be sure just how many of Nusair's people are running around out there that you'll need security twenty-four/seven."

Catching her breath was suddenly impossible. "But my work is here…yours is—"

"Wherever I chose." He dragged off his jacket. "I thought I might buy a place here. Maybe on the Sound. Personally handle your case."

She loved watching him take off his jacket like that. There was something incredibly sexy about it. "That would be…great." Puget Sound… beautiful place, but right now all she could do was look at him and wish they were someplace private.

"I might have to spend the occasional day in D.C. Maybe you could manage a day off now and then."

"That could probably be arranged," she ventured, her heart already thumping wildly in her chest. "Cooperation is my middle name."

He loosened his tie. "I'm counting on that."

Her pulse reacted as she watched his fingers undo a couple of buttons at his throat.

When he walked toward her, she held up her hands to halt him. "Okay, I can't take this." Her gaze collided with his. "Where *exactly* is this headed, Krueger?"

"Anywhere you want to go." He took one of her hands in his and pulled her closer. "I'll be happy to let you lead."

Then he kissed her. Kissed her until her heart flailed impotently.

He drew back just far enough for her to draw in a desperately needed breath. "I've been looking for you my whole life, Claire."

Oh, God. Of all the things he could have said, that was the one line that could actually get to her. "Krueger, I—"

"Luke," he whispered before brushing his lips over hers.

Then he kissed her again.

By the time he stopped she was pretty sure they were going to have to get a room.

"Luke," she murmured against his lips, "we… ah…"

"Will continue this at the nearest hotel," he suggested, those skilled lips doing wild and wicked things to her skin as he traced a path along the curve of her neck.

"I can't leave the hospital until Darlene is out of recovery." She moaned…couldn't help herself. She wanted to be with him so much. His hands were moving along the length of her spine, molding to every rise and hollow. Her head was spinning.

He pressed his forehead to hers. "Okay. As soon as she's out of the woods and your sister is settled in somewhere that meets your approval, we are going to finish this."

She smiled. "Definitely."

His mouth closed over hers once more and the ability to think disappeared.

Now this was definitely worth *almost* dying for…over and over again.

* * * * *

Happily ever after is just the beginning...

Turn the page for a sneak preview of
DANCING ON SUNDAY AFTERNOONS
by
Linda Cardillo.

Harlequin Everlasting—Every great love
has a story to tell. ™
A brand-new line from Harlequin Books
launching this February!

PROLOGUE

Giulia D'Orazio
1983

I had two husbands—Paolo and Salvatore.

Salvatore and I were married for thirty-two years. I still live in the house he bought for us. I still sleep in our bed. All around me are the signs of our life together. My bedroom window looks out over the garden he planted. In the middle of the city, he coaxed tomatoes, peppers, zucchini— even grapes for his wine—out of the ground. On weekends, he used to drive up to his cousin's farm in Waterbury and bring back manure. In the winter, he wrapped the peach tree and the fig tree with rags and black rubber hoses against the cold, his massive, coarse hands gentling those trees as if they were his fragile-skinned babies. My neighbor, Dominic Grazza, does that for me now. My boys have no time for the garden.

In the front of the house, Salvatore planted roses. The roses I take care of myself. They are giant, cream colored, fragrant. In the afternoons, I like to sit out on the porch with my coffee, protected from the eyes of the neighborhood by that curtain of flowers.

Salvatore died in this house thirty-five years ago. In the last months, he lay on the sofa in the parlor so he could be in the middle of everything. Except for the two oldest boys, all the children were still at home and we ate together every evening. Salvatore could see the dining room table from the sofa and he could hear everything that was said. "I'm not dead, yet," he told me. "I want to know what's going on."

When my first grandchild, Cara, was born, we brought her to him, and he held her on his chest, stroking her tiny head. Sometimes they fell asleep together.

Over on the radiator cover in the corner of the parlor is the portrait Salvatore and I had taken on our twenty-fifth anniversary. This brooch I'm wearing today, with the diamonds—I'm wearing it in the photograph also—Salvatore gave it to me that day. Upstairs on my dresser is a jewelry box filled with necklaces and bracelets and earrings. All from Salvatore.

I am surrounded by the things Salvatore gave me, or did for me. But, God forgive me, as I lie alone now in my bed, it is Paolo I remember.

Paolo left me nothing. Nothing, that is, that my family, especially my sisters, thought had any value. No house. No diamonds. Not even a photograph.

But after he was gone and I could catch my breath from the pain, I knew that I still had something. In the middle of the night, I sat alone and held them in my hands, reading the words over and over until I heard his voice in my head. I had Paolo's letters.

* * * * *

*Be sure to look for DANCING ON SUNDAY
AFTERNOONS
available January 30, 2007.
And look, too, for our other Everlasting
title available,
FALL FROM GRACE by Kristi Gold.*

*FALL FROM GRACE is a deeply emotional story
of what a long-term love really means.
As Jack and Anne Morgan discover,
marriage vows can be broken—
but they can be mended, too.
And the memories of their marriage
have an unexpected power
to bring back a love that never really left....*

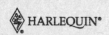

EVERLASTING LOVE™

Every great love has a story to tell™

Save $1.⁰⁰ off

**the purchase of
any Harlequin
Everlasting Love novel**

Coupon valid from January 1, 2007
until April 30, 2007.

Valid at retail outlets in the U.S. only.
Limit one coupon per customer.

RETAILER: Harlequin Enterprises Limited will pay the face value of this coupon plus
8¢ if submitted by the customer for this product only. Any other use constitutes fraud.
Coupon is nonassignable. Void if taxed, prohibited or restricted by law. Consumer
must pay any government taxes. Void if copied. For reimbursement submit coupons
and proof of sales directly to: Harlequin Enterprises Ltd., P.O. Box 880478, El Paso,
TX 88588-0478, U.S.A. Cash value 1/100¢. Valid in the U.S. only. ® is a trademark of
Harlequin Enterprises Ltd. Trademarks marked with ® are registered in the United
States and/or other countries.

5 65373 00076 2   (8100)0 11302

HEUSCPN0407

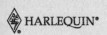

HARLEQUIN®

EVERLASTING LOVE™

Every great love has a story to tell™

Fall from Grace

Kristi Gold

Save $1.⁰⁰ off

the purchase of
any Harlequin
Everlasting Love novel

Coupon valid from January 1, 2007
until April 30, 2007.

Valid at retail outlets in Canada only.
Limit one coupon per customer.

52607370

HECDNCPN0407

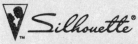

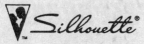

Romantic
SUSPENSE

Excitement, danger and passion guaranteed!

Same great authors and riveting editorial
you've come to know and love
from Silhouette Intimate Moments.

> *New York Times*
> bestselling author
> Beverly Barton
> is back with the
> latest installment
> in her popular
> miniseries,
> The Protectors.
> HIS ONLY
> OBSESSION
> is available
> next month from
> Silhouette®
> Romantic Suspense

Look for it wherever you buy books!